# STARGÅTE SG·1™

# BEHIND ENEMY LINES

## Sally Malcolm

# FANDEMONIUM BOOKS

An original publication of Fandemonium Ltd, produced under license from MGM Consumer Products.

Fandemonium Books
United Kingdom
Visit our website: www.stargatenovels.com

# STARGATE SG·1

METRO-GOLDWYN-MAYER Presents
STARGATE SG-1™
BEN BROWDER  AMANDA TAPPING  CHRISTOPHER JUDGE  CLAUDIA BLACK
with BEAU BRIDGES and MICHAEL SHANKS as Daniel Jackson
Executive Producers ROBERT C. COOPER & BRAD WRIGHT
Developed for Television by BRAD WRIGHT & JONATHAN GLASSNER



WWW.MGM.COM

Print ISBN: 978-1-905586-80-6   Ebook ISBN: 978-1-80070-063-5

**Author's note**

This story is set in 2013, ten years after the season seven episode STARGATE SG-1: *Fragile Balance* and one year after my short story, *Off Balance,* first published in our anthology STARGATE: Far Horizons.

*Off Balance* is included as a prologue for those who haven't read it.

# PROLOGUE

## STARGATE SG-1: *Off Balance*

This prologue was first published as a short story in our anthology **STARGATE:** *Far Horizons* and provides the back story to the novella, *Behind Enemy Lines,* which begins with chapter one.

COMING out of the bend, he opened the throttle and smiled as the bike leapt forward, eating up the empty road. Adrenaline kicked, the needle nosed over ninety, and the thrill of all that raw power brought him alive for a precious few seconds.

Cliffs soared high on his right, sunset casting the rock in shades of burnt orange, turning the landscape alien, otherworldly. And he should know.

He felt a spike of loss — still keen after nine years — and accelerated harder, just to blast the feeling away. He liked speed, he'd always liked speed. His wife had once told him, with a note of fond exasperation, that he was born to be a flyboy. The memory still made him smile, though it was long ago now, part of his lost life.

Up ahead, he could see a line of mountains — the Collegiate Peaks — and the glitter of Buena Vista's lights scattered through the evening shadows. He'd almost topped ninety-five, and was just throttling back, when he heard the siren wail behind him.

Crap.

He slowed, glanced in the mirror and saw the flashing lights of the patrol car pulling him over. Obeying orders was in his blood and, besides, he knew the drill; this wasn't the first time he'd encountered Colorado's finest. Pulling onto the shoulder, he killed the engine and tugged off his helmet. He'd never been good at feigning contrition, but he did his best as the officer climbed out of his car. Recent experience had taught him that cops didn't like kids with smart mouths.

Tall, lanky, maybe early thirties, the police officer walked with a youthful swagger — the kind of bravado born of a uniform, a rank, and a gun at your side. "You know why I stopped you, son?" the cop said.

"Yes sir." He hated being called 'son' by kids almost half his age.

"I'm gonna need to see your driver's license."

He handed it over and the officer studied it for a moment, then peered at him over the tops of his sunglasses. "Jonathan O'Neill."

"Yes sir."

"You go by Jack?"

"Used to," he said. "Not anymore."

The officer didn't comment, eyes hidden again behind his dark glasses. "Is this your bike, son?"

"Yes sir."

"BMW R1200GS? That's a lotta machine for a kid your age."

He gave a little shrug. "I'm older than I look."

"Says here you're twenty-four. And that's an expensive bike."

"It was a gift," he said, "from my uncle. Uncle Samuel."

And, all things considered, that wasn't exactly a lie. He had to do something with the guilt money that dutifully rolled in each month from the Air Force.

As usually happened, the police officer walked away a few steps and spoke into his radio, probably calling through a check to make sure the bike wasn't stolen and that 'Jonathan O'Neill' wasn't wanted for grand theft auto across all fifty states. Everything came back clean, of course, and in the end he only had to endure a lecture on responsibility from a guy who had no idea what responsibility meant.

It was dusk by the time he was allowed to go, so he turned around and headed back toward Salida. He was a little surprised that the police car followed him all the way into town, only moving on after he'd pulled into the parking lot outside Bosco's Tavern. He guessed the cop didn't have much else to do, and resisted the urge to wave him goodbye. Low-profile was the watchword of his so-called life these days, and sassing the police wouldn't help keep him out of trouble.

Bosco's was dimly lit with plenty of corners to hide in. Jack knew it well; he often came here when he was out riding and he liked its shadows. They made it easy to hide. The food was good too, and he ordered a steak and a beer and ate slowly, trying not to think about much of anything. It was an art he'd perfected during his years in exile. Don't think about what's happening out there in the big wide galaxy, because there's nothing you can do about it anymore. Don't think about whether the people you care about are alive or dead, because you'll probably never know. Don't think about your family, your ex-wife, your lost son — all of them belong to someone else. Don't think about any of it, just live in the moment.

Behind him, he heard a swell of voices — an argument brewing, then fading away. He glanced over his shoulder and saw a woman and a man at the pool table, her with hands on hips and him drunk and unpleasant. Ignoring them, Jack turned back to his meal and took a long swallow of cold beer. It helped that he could buy himself a drink now, even if he was still carded a lot of the time. He'd always looked young for his age, ironically.

But at least the face he saw in the mirror these days was starting to look familiar again. He remembered this face, remembered being this guy. There were fewer scars this time around, but his life since leaving the SGC had been a lot less interesting. The last time he'd been twenty-four, he'd already been a serving officer, a pilot. He'd seen combat. This time? Well, it turned out that after you'd spent seven years on the galactic frontline it was difficult to feel like much else in the world really mattered.

The argument behind him grew louder, but he didn't turn

back around despite his instinct to step in. He'd learned to control that impulse, too, over the past few years. Yet the rise and fall of arguing voices threaded their way through the music, a baseline of unease that made him edgy. Perhaps that's why he was on alert when the bar door opened and two men in dark suits entered. He clocked them immediately, watching as they took seats at the bar, ordered drinks, and glanced around the room with feigned indifference. He didn't recognize their faces, but they had military intelligence stamped all over them. A prickle of tension ran along the back of his neck, half disquiet and half excitement. Were they here for him, after all this time? Was he in danger? Was he needed?

"Son of a bitch!" The shout came from behind him, rolled up in a huge crash and a woman's scream.

Jack was on his feet in an instant — just in time to see a man go flying across the pool table, and another leap over it after him, a pool cue clutched like a club. A bottle broke and there was blood. Jack couldn't stop himself.

"Hey!" he yelled, running over. No one paid any attention, the woman was still screaming and the man with the cue in his hand was hammering at the other guy who lay curled in a ball on the floor.

"That's my goddamn wife, you sonofa —"

"Hey!" Jack grabbed the attacker's arm, twisted it behind him until he dropped the cue with a yell, and then turned him fast and shoved him face down onto the pool table. He held him there. "Cool it," he ordered.

The attacker was drunk and obstreperous. "What the — ?"

Jack jerked his arm higher, making him grunt in pain. "I said cool it, buddy."

The other man staggered to his feet. There was a gash on his head, blood dripping down his face and into his eyes. He looked dizzy, like he was about to faint or throw up.

"Sit down," Jack barked at him. "You," he said to the woman, "help him."

She stared at him through clumpy black lashes and a fall of hair too blonde for her middle-aged skin. "Look, kid—"

"Do it," he demanded, like she was a new recruit. "Now."

She blinked, but few people could ignore orders given in that tone of voice. He'd spent years perfecting the ideal balance of threat, demand, and expectation. It worked every time, and this was no exception. She helped the guy sit down, watching Jack as if she weren't sure what to make of him.

Then there were staff everywhere and the manager was threatening to call the cops. Jack realized he still had the guy pinned to the pool table and let go, aware of too many curious eyes on him. Heading back to his table, he grabbed his jacket and left before the manager could rope him into talking to the police.

He was halfway across the parking lot when he noticed the car. A black sedan lurked at the far side of the lot, as out of place as the two suits had been in the bar. His blood was still up from the fight, senses heightened, and he knew there was something wrong here. Instinct urged him to run, to grab a weapon and prepare for an ambush. But he had no weapon, so he just kept walking toward his bike, hairs rising on the back of his neck. He'd barely taken half a dozen steps when someone behind him spoke.

"Colonel O'Neill."

He stopped dead. Keeping it nonchalant, Jack turned around. "You got the wrong guy," he said to the suit standing behind him.

"I don't think so, sir." The man took a step forward. Jack recognized him from earlier, in the bar. "Apologies for approaching you like this, Colonel, but we need your help."

Jack glanced around, but the parking lot was empty. "And who's 'we', exactly?"

"The Pentagon, sir. Homeworld Security."

He raised an eyebrow. "Home*world* Security? Never heard of them."

"A lot's changed since you left the program, sir." The suit gestured toward the car. "Please, we don't have long to fill you in."

He glanced over at the sedan, all dark windows and bullet-proof glass. His bike was about twenty yards behind him. He could make it in a couple of seconds, could probably outrun the car. "You know," he said, "my mom always told me not to get into cars with strangers."

The suit nodded and reached into his breast pocket. Jack swallowed and managed not to reach for a weapon that wasn't there. "Major Kevin Hartkans, sir." The man pulled out his military ID and held it up. "Pentagon."

It looked real, but you could forge anything these days. Jack licked his lips, thinking it through. This moment — the recall to active duty — was something he'd longed for ever since he'd left the SGC. And yet… "Where's General Hammond?"

Hartkans's face tightened. "Sir, I regret to inform you that General Hammond passed away two years ago."

It knocked the air right out of him. All he could manage to say was, "How?"

"A heart attack, sir."

He felt a swift, hot flare of anger. George Hammond was gone — had been gone for two years — and Jack hadn't even *known*? They hadn't even let him pay his last respects.

Hartkans glanced again at the car. "Colonel, I'm sorry, but we don't have much time. If you could come with me, I can brief you fully on the situation on our way."

But he wasn't going anywhere, not yet. Not until he knew. "My team," he said in a voice steadier than he felt. "SG-1?"

With a shake of his head, Hartkans lowered his voice and took a step closer. "That's why I'm here, sir."

His stomach plummeted into his boots. "Tell me."

In the dark of the parking lot, Hartkans's face was all shadows. "They're in trouble, Colonel. And they need your help."

"Yup," Daniel said, peering through his binoculars, "we're in trouble."

Teal'c shifted where he crouched next to Daniel. "There appear to be many Oranians converging on this site."

"Yeah, like I said: we're in trouble."

"Well, perhaps they're not here looking for the same thing we are?" Vala suggested. "I mean look at this place — sunshine, ocean. Wonderful views."

Daniel cast a look over his shoulder. "You think they're tourists?"

"I'm saying they might be."

"With guns?"

She shrugged. "It's a dangerous galaxy, Daniel."

Trying not to roll his eyes, he turned back to the road below. There were twenty Oranians, maybe more, in a tight-packed group, heavily armed, with a few outriders serving as scouts. And they were heading directly for the Ancient outpost.

"Looks to me," Mitchell said, "like they know exactly what they're after."

"We cannot permit them to retrieve the device," Teal'c said. "If it were to fall into the hands of the Lucian Alliance…"

No one needed to hear the end of that sentence. The Alliance might have been weakened after their failed attack on Earth, but no one doubted their commitment to removing the Tau'ri threat from the galaxy. And this device might be able to do exactly that.

"So," Mitchell said, "I guess we find the thing before they do."

"Oh good," said Vala, smiling up at the Ancient outpost towering above them. "I do love a treasure hunt."

The empty warehouse, on the outskirts of Colorado Springs, looked nothing like the Pentagon. Jack eyed it suspiciously through the tinted glass of the sedan as it rolled to a stop in the deserted parking lot of the industrial park.

"Don't worry, Colonel," Hartkans said. "This isn't our base of operations."

"Okay," he said, reserving judgment. The driver got out, came around, and opened the door for him with a crisp salute. Jack couldn't deny that it felt good to be accorded the respect of rank again; he hadn't realized how much he'd missed it.

He nodded to the airman as he climbed out, tugged down at the hem of his shirt and wished he had a uniform. "So," he said to Hartkans, "now what?"

The major indicated a small door, light seeping out from around its edges. "This way, sir."

Inside, there were a few boxes, and some communications equipment, and a couple of airmen studying computer screens. They jumped to their feet when Jack approached, coming to attention. "Sir," one of them said to Hartkans. "*Avenger* reports ready."

"Thank you, Phillips." Hartkans turned to Jack. "Stand by for transport, sir."

"Transport? Where are we — ?"

The fall of Goa'uld transport rings cut off the question and in a flare of white light he was somewhere else. Dropping into a defensive crouch, he had to blink several times to make sense of what he saw. He was on a Goa'uld ship, but the people standing looking at him were no Jaffa. They were human, most dressed in the mishmash of leather and sackcloth he associated with off-world populations. Some, though, were in uniform — USAF uniform — and one of them stepped forward.

"Colonel O'Neill," he said. "Relax, you're among friends."

Straightening, but not lowering his guard, Jack took in the stars on the man's shoulder. "General... ?"

"Turner. We haven't met." He gave a thin smile. "That is, I've only met *General* O'Neill."

"You're kidding," Jack said, surprised. "He took a desk job?"

Turner spread his hands, declining to comment. "Let's find you a uniform," he said. "We have a lot to do."

"Yeah, about that," Jack said, glancing around and trying to get a feel for what the hell was going on. "I can't help noticing we're on a Goa'uld mothership."

The general smiled again. "*Former* Goa'uld mothership," he said, gesturing for Jack to walk with him as Hartkans led the way through the corridors of the ha'tak. "We got hold of a number of them after the fall of the System Lords."

"Excuse me?" Jack almost missed a step. "It sounded like you said 'the fall of the System Lords'."

"Yes, Colonel, that's exactly what I said."

"As in… all of them?"

Turner smiled again. "Every last one — even Ba'al, in the end."

"Okay," he said, blindsided. They'd won the war and no one had told him. No one had told him Ba'al was dead. "I guess I didn't get the memo."

"In here, Colonel." Hartkans stopped in front of an open door, through which Jack could see a neatly folded uniform sitting on top of a narrow cot. "These are your quarters, sir."

Jack didn't enter. "Nine years," he said to Turner. "I've been out in the cold for nine years. No one told me George Hammond died. No one told me we won the war against the Goa'uld. No one told me that Ba'al —" He bit that off, uncomfortable with the way it made his voice tighten. There was an awkward silence. Turner clearly didn't know what to say, and Jack guessed this wasn't really his fault. He threw him a bone. "All these years, and nothing — why should I help you now?"

It was Hartkans who answered. "Because you're Colonel Jack O'Neill, sir, and your team needs you."

He turned back to the doorway, to the uniform that lay beyond. He could see the patch on the jacket sleeve: SG-1. "What about the other guy?" he said. "It's his team, not mine."

"General O'Neill left the SGC a number of years ago," Hartkans said. "He's now head of Homeworld Security."

Jack almost laughed. "Well that's ridiculous. I'd never —"

"Colonel," Turner snapped, "put the uniform on and consider yourself recalled to active duty." He looked at Hartkans.

"Bring him to the briefing as soon as he's ready."

With that, he stalked away leaving Jack hovering on the threshold. This was what he'd longed for: a recall to active duty, to the life that had been taken from him. And yet. And yet…

"Sir?" Hartkans said. "We don't have much time."

*And I don't have much choice.* There was no way he would pass up this chance.

At first glance the Ancient outpost looked like a ruin, weathered and crumbling where it perched like a gothic dream on the cliff edge. Its melancholy air appealed to the romantic in Daniel, but, as usual, he didn't have time to relish it or to absorb the architectural wonders on display. The way Ancient structures seemed to defy physics was something he'd often considered, in passing, but had never had time to really pursue. Perhaps one day, when they were all too old to do this anymore, he'd sit down with Sam and figure out exactly how they whisked up the confections of spires and turrets that marked so much of their architecture.

The thought made him smile — a smile that was nudged off his face by Vala elbowing him in the ribs. "Wake up," she said. "We're here."

'Here' was the entrance they'd discovered on their first recon of the planet: a doorway that led down into the preserved lower half of the structure. Carved — again, he'd have to ask Sam how they'd done it — into the solid stone of the cliff, the rooms below were shielded from the elements and remained intact. And it was somewhere in this labyrinth of tunnels and stairways that the device they were searching for lay hidden. At least, that's what Vala's map, and the scan run by the *Daedalus,* told them.

Cam pulled off his sunglasses and peered into the darkness. "We'll need a flashlight," he said.

Daniel smiled at the understatement. "You know," he said, as he reached into his vest for his headlamp, "even if the Oranians do find the device, they won't be able to use it. And, most likely, neither will the Lucian Alliance."

"All they need is someone with the ATA gene," Cam said. "And they're not so hard to find these days."

"Maybe." Daniel switched on his lamp, turning his head so as not to blind the others. "But for a device capable of exterminating an entire species? The Ancients were careful. I'd be surprised if a weakly or artificially expressed ATA gene would be enough to activate it. And there aren't so many Ancients in the Milky Way these days."

"Either way," Cam said, "I'd rather blow the thing up. Just in case."

Daniel didn't argue with that. Ancient or not, some things didn't deserve preservation.

"I'll take point." Cam switched on his weapon's tactical flashlight, sweeping it across the staircase leading down into the dark. "Vala, show me the map."

"Right here," she said, with the childlike enthusiasm Daniel somehow found both captivating and infuriating. He wanted to tell her that this wasn't a game, it wasn't a treasure hunt… but of course she knew that as well as any of them. This was just her way of dealing. He'd found Jack's irreverence in the face of certain doom equally exasperating.

"Okay," Cam said, looking up from the map. "Vala, stick with me. Teal'c — watch our six. I don't want those Oranians creeping up on us." He glanced at Daniel. "Let's go."

Like everything on the ship, the briefing room was a kaleidoscopic mix of different people, technologies and cultures. A table that might have been lifted from a Pentagon meeting room dominated the space, at odds with the gaudy Goa'uld décor, and around it sat a group of hard-faced people much like those he'd passed in the corridors on the way from his quarters.

When Jack arrived, Turner was in close conversation with another man, tall and lanky. He wasn't in uniform, but his clothes looked like they came from Earth and not the Leather Emporium that seemed to outfit the rest of the galaxy. They turned when Jack and Hartkans entered, and Jack recognized the stranger immediately as the cop who'd pulled him over that night.

"Small world," Jack said.

He got an apologetic smile in response. "Sorry, Colonel, but we needed visual confirmation that you were who we thought you were."

"Take a seat, Jack," Turner said, cutting through the small talk.

He did, keeping a wary eye on the disreputable-looking people opposite. None of them appeared friendly.

"You're the Asgard clone?" a woman said abruptly. She was strongly built, with hard eyes and hair pulled back from an angular face.

"Among other things," Jack said. "And you are…?"

"Balen Tark. This is my ship." She gave him a brazen, appreciative look. "What do you call yourself?"

He hesitated over his first name, like he often did, and settled on, "O'Neill. You can call me O'Neill."

She tossed him a smile, full of teeth. "And what do you want to call me?"

It felt like a loaded question and he had no idea how to respond. Luckily, Turner interrupted.

"Let's get this started," he said, and gestured toward Jack. "As you can see, we've located the —" He cut himself off. "That is, Colonel O'Neill has agreed to help us." He turned to the fake cop. "Devon, give us the rundown, please."

Devon, it turned out, was the Daniel Jackson of the outfit — complete with PowerPoint presentation. "Colonel," he said, addressing Jack directly, "what you probably don't know about yourself is that you possess what we call the Ancient Technology Activation gene, or the ATA gene."

"Catchy name."

Devon smiled, but didn't miss a beat. "The gene — which is very strongly expressed in you — allows you to activate a number of technologies left behind by the Ancients. Now, we've developed a retrovirus that can activate—"

"Devon?" Turner interrupted. "Cut to the chase, will you?"

Devon cleared his throat, frowned, and said, "Yes sir. We've recently discovered an Ancient device that's capable of exterminating an entire species. However, it's clear that the Ancients didn't want this to fall into general use. We think, perhaps, that it was an attempt to find a weapon to combat the Wraith."

"The what?" Jack said.

Turner waved the question away. "Not pertinent to this mission, Colonel."

"The point is," Devon continued, "that we believe only someone with a very strong, naturally expressed ATA gene can make the device work. And we think that's you, Colonel."

"And why would I want to activate a device that can exterminate anything?" he said. "Except maybe mosquitoes. We're not talking about mosquitoes, are we?"

Turner leaned forward, hands braced on the table; he wasn't blessed with a great sense of humor, Jack decided. "You want to activate it, Colonel," he said, "because it's the only way to save your team."

Jack took a moment to absorb that assertion, but kept his face neutral. "By exterminating an entire *species*?"

"Colonel," Turner said, "the creatures holding SG-1 are vicious. They *will* kill them, eventually. But before that…"

He left it hanging and Jack didn't need to imagine the rest. He shifted, feeling uncomfortable — and not just because the seat was hard. "You're gonna need to explain this, General."

Irritation flickered across Turner's face. "SG-1 was sent on a mission to destroy the device, but an Oranian faction got there first and captured them. They're using them as a bargaining chip to leave the planet with the device. Our mission is to stop them."

"With extreme prejudice, I assume?"

"A conventional incursion wouldn't stand a chance, Jack. They'd kill SG-1 as soon as the offensive began. But if a small team could infiltrate the outpost and activate the device…" He gave a quick, nasty smile. "They're all dead and SG-1 walk free."

"How does it work?"

Devon brightened up. "That's a good question, sir. We think that it —"

"It uses DNA," Turner said, talking right over him. "We've calibrated it to Oranian DNA, but the Ancients designed the device so that only one of them — someone with the ATA gene — could initiate the weapon."

Jack scrubbed a hand through his hair, considering the story. "Why me?" he said eventually. "Why not him? The other O'Neill." The real one.

Devon and Turner exchanged a furtive look. "Okay," Turner said after a moment, "I'll level with you, Jack."

"Well, that would be nice."

"This isn't exactly official," Turner admitted. "We've been authorized to operate below the radar."

Jack sat back in his chair, tension tight down the length of his spine. It wasn't that he'd completely trusted these people in the first place, but he couldn't deny that he'd really *wanted* to believe that this was the call he'd been hoping for. He swallowed his disappointment and tried not to look like he was on full alert. "So who are you?" he said, looking around the table. "NID? Is Kinsey behind this?"

Turner shook his head. "Kinsey's dead."

"Convenient. Seems like everyone I know is either dead or missing."

"It's been a long nine years," Turner said. "And if we'd had a choice, we wouldn't have recalled you. But we don't. You're no stranger to covert operations, Colonel. Sometimes it's the only way."

He couldn't argue with that, but something still didn't sit right. He caught a tense glance between Turner and the woman, Balen Tark. "And what do you get out of this?" he asked her.

"The Oranians have killed many of our people," she said, leaning back in her chair as if she were about to prop her feet on the table. "My ship isn't called the *Avenger* for nothing, O'Neill."

"You're talking about a weapon of mass destruction."

"By any means necessary, Colonel," Turner said. "You know that."

He did know that, but he also wished he had Daniel here to argue the other corner. Daniel wasn't here, though; he was being held prisoner along with the rest of his team. Apparently.

"Look," Turner said, "how do you think we tracked you down?"

"Facebook?"

Turner's lips pressed into an unamused line. "General O'Neill told us where to find you. He'd be here himself, if he could, but in his position…" He spread his hands. "Jack, look around you. The galaxy's changed. It's not as simple as it was when the Goa'uld had everything locked down. In many ways, it's even more dangerous out here."

In truth, Jack had no way of knowing whether Turner was on the level. He wasn't sure he bought the story that his alter ego was the Big Man in DC. In fact, he wasn't sure he bought a lot of what they were selling him. He was out of his depth and he didn't like it. But he wasn't about to let on, so all he said was, "After we do this, what happens to the device?"

"We destroy it." Perhaps Turner said it a little too fast, or perhaps it was the way his gaze flickered toward Balen Tark, but Jack wasn't sure he believed that either.

He looked at the woman, but her expression was opaque. Jack didn't miss the tense line of her shoulders, however, or the fact that the whole room was holding its breath. He made himself lean back in his chair, look relaxed. "What if I won't do it?"

Turner's expression was flinty. "Then you'd be disobeying a direct order, Colonel."

"I'm not him," he said. "I'm not 'Colonel O'Neill'. You can't give me orders."

"I thought you'd have more loyalty to your team, Jack."

"The SG-1 I knew wouldn't want me to commit mass murder on their behalf. In fact, the Jack O'Neill I knew wouldn't be too happy about it either."

Turner steepled his fingers on the table, letting a moment pass. "You want to go back to drinking alone in seedy bars, Jack? Getting your kicks from riding too fast on the interstate? Because I can send you back there. If you don't have the stomach for this, I can send you back to that life."

Jack held his gaze, trying to get the measure of the man. He wasn't having much luck.

"Or you can stay and help," Turner said. "You can get back into the action, make a difference again. Save your team. Save Earth."

"And then what? Back on the scrap heap?"

Turner shook his head. "We'll find a place for you. The Stargate Program's gotten a whole lot bigger than just the SGC. There are plenty of places where a man of your talents and experience could make himself useful. Hell, there are whole new *galaxies* to explore."

"Is that so?"

"You wouldn't believe what's out here, Jack."

And that was exactly the problem. Hammond and Kinsey were dead? SG-1 was in trouble? The Goa'uld had been destroyed? He — the real Jack O'Neill — was heading up the whole operation from DC? How the hell was he supposed to know what to believe?

He didn't trust Balen Tark, or Devon, or any of them. But Turner was right about one thing: this was a chance to get back into the game, to reclaim something of the life he'd lost. So maybe these guys were NID, or something else shadowy, but maybe that didn't matter. He'd lived as a shadow for a decade anyway, a ghost of himself. Maybe it was time he started salvaging what he could of his life.

He fixed Turner with a hard look, trying not to hear Daniel's warning voice in the back of his head as he said, "So where do we find this doomsday machine?"

"Damn," Cam said, crouching low against the wall and releasing a precise burst of weapons fire up the staircase. "They got here fast."

"You'd be amazed what Oranians can do when they smell profit," Vala said.

"We cannot hold them here." Teal'c was farther down the narrow stairway, wielding his flashlight to try and see into the darkness. "There appears to be a room to the left, less than a hundred meters away."

"We don't want to get trapped," Cam warned.

"Better than dead," Vala said.

Daniel stood up, staying flat against the wall. "Teal'c and I can check it out, see if there's a back door."

Cam nodded, not taking his eyes off the Oranians further up the stairs. "Be quick, or we'll be falling back anyway."

With a nod at Teal'c, Daniel began to run down the steep steps. Teal'c was right; there was a door, and the panel at its side looked like it would open it if there were power. He jabbed at it anyway, to no effect. Behind him, Cam's P90 rattled again, overlaid by the electronic hiss of Vala's zat.

"Any ideas?" Daniel said.

Teal'c just gave him a look. "Stand back, Daniel Jackson." His roundhouse kick looked terrifying, but his foot impacted harmlessly on the door. With a growl, Teal'c threw his shoulder against it. Still nothing.

Daniel's radio crackled. "We're falling back."

Damn it. "Fall back slowly!"

He looked at the panel again. "There must be a manual override," he said. "There must be a way to open a door if the power goes out, right?"

"Perhaps," Teal'c said, rubbing his shoulder.

Daniel got closer to the wall, scanning its surface with his eyes and fingers, looking for irregularities. Ancient design was smooth, sinuous, and it was only as he traced it with his fingertips that he felt the slight ridge in the surface that cut across the whorls. "There's another panel here," he said, and wished Sam was with them. He pressed it and, to his surprise, it moved inward and then opened with a slow slide. Inside there was a simple lever, which he pulled, and the door released and slid open a few inches. "Yes," he breathed.

Jamming his fingers into the gap, Teal'c hauled it open. Daylight flooded out from the small room on the other side, its narrow window looking out over the ocean. Daniel figured that counted as a backdoor. "Cam," he said into his radio, "come on down. There's a way out."

"On our way," Mitchell replied. "So are the Oranians."

Teal'c covered the door, firing back up the stairs as Vala and Cam retreated into the room, then Teal'c pushed at the door, muscles bunching as it slid shut with a click.

"It won't take them long to figure out how to open it," Daniel pointed out.

Two quick shots from Vala's zat left the door mechanism smoking. "Now no one can open it," she said.

Daniel didn't comment on the obvious flaw in her plan.

Cam was peering out the window, still catching his breath from his flight down the stairs. "When you said there was a way out…"

Daniel joined him at the window and gazed down at the glittering ocean. "Hmm," he said. "That's a long drop."

"I sure hope someone brought a rope."

The boom of ocean waves crashing against a cliff face greeted them as they stepped out of the Stargate onto P3X-406, the glare of sunlight on water almost blinding. Jack wished he still had his trusty glacier sunglasses, but that was something else the other O'Neill had kept for himself.

"Spread out," said Balen Tark, and he watched as her people fanned out around the gate, securing the perimeter. They were good, whoever they were. Jack didn't move, though, still savoring the sensation of gate travel — the indefinable frisson of stepping through the event horizon and launching yourself across the galaxy. Damn, but he'd missed it.

Ahead, perching on the cliffs that fell away a hundred meters to the left of the Stargate, stood the Ancient outpost. Gray as the rock it was built on, it nonetheless had something of a fairytale aspect as it teetered over the ocean, its spires glittering in the planet's hot sun. Jack figured there'd be one heck of a view from the guest rooms.

"No welcoming committee?" he said to Hartkans, who stood next to him on the stone steps.

"Oranians are a spacefaring race," Hartkans said. "They rarely use Stargates. They prefer to land a ship instead."

"That's new," said Jack, and tugged the standard issue ball cap lower over his eyes. He missed his own kit. Without it he felt like he was just playing at being Colonel O'Neill. The only things in his pockets that he actually owned were his wallet and the keys to his bike, still parked outside Bosco's Tavern. But the P90 was familiar, at least, and he relished the feel of it in his hands after so long. Until he'd put on the uniform and stepped through the Stargate, he hadn't realized how disconnected he'd become from the man he'd once been.

"You're sure you know what to do, Colonel?" Hartkans said, flinching slightly as the wormhole disengaged behind them.

"It's not difficult," Jack said. "We get into the outpost and find the device. I activate it — killing the Oranians — and then we spring SG-1 from jail." *Assuming they're still alive. Assuming any of this is true.* "What could possibly go wrong?"

Hartkans didn't answer. "Balen," he said instead, "leave some of your people to hold the gate, just in case."

"In case of what?" Jack said.

Hartkans walked down the steps, away from the Stargate, without looking over his shoulder. "In case something unexpected happens."

Jack had a feeling Hartkans was expecting something unexpected.

There'd been a time when rappelling down the outside of an Ancient structure on an alien world would have been a remarkable event, but that time was long past. Now, as Teal'c grabbed hold of his wrist and helped him climb in through the window, what Daniel mostly felt was tired.

"Thanks," he said, shaking loose the cramps in his arms and rolling his shoulders. Vala sat some distance away, back against the wall, chewing on a power bar while Mitchell was studying the door. The room they were in was larger than the one above, with an annex through an archway off to the right.

"Bathroom," Vala said, when she saw Daniel looking. "En suite. No water, though. I checked."

"No power either?" Daniel guessed.

"And no way out," Mitchell confirmed, turning away from the door. "Unless you can open this one too?"

"I can try," Daniel said.

He found the manual override without much trouble, but it was broken. The lever wobbled and was obviously no longer connected to the door mechanism. Daniel sat back on his heels. "So, plan B?"

Teal'c was still at the window, one hand on the rope as if he could will it to detach itself and fall down. "I could attempt to free climb back up and retrieve the rope," he speculated, but Cam shut him down with a wave of his hand.

"We have C4," he said. "We'll just blow the door."

"Well, *that* won't tell the Oranians exactly where to find us," Vala said.

Cam fixed her with a look. "You got a better plan?"

Turned out, for once, she didn't.

The sun was hot — he'd forgotten how alien suns could be hotter or colder than Earth's Goldilocks star — but Jack found he didn't much mind the heat as they took the path from the gate to the outpost. There were definite advantages to this young body he'd inherited: endurance, strength, and undamaged knees were some of the most noticeable. He figured, physically, he was even younger than Daniel and Carter had been when they'd first joined the SGC. Mentally, though, he felt as wise as Methuselah.

An experienced mind in a young body made a potent combination, which was probably why he recognized the approaching sound before the others — the scuffing of boots against rock. "Off the path," he hissed, ducking behind one of the boulders that littered the cliff top.

The creatures who marched past were like nothing he'd seen before. They certainly weren't human. Their faces were reptilian, long and with weird tentacles on either side. There was a group of about five of them, heavily armed, escorting a ragged human prisoner. He glanced at Balen, who was watching them with narrowed eyes and a twitchy trigger finger.

She spared him a look and in a low voice said, "Oranian hunting dogs."

"Dangerous?"

Her grin was savage. "What do you think?"

Jack preferred to keep his thoughts to himself, so he said, "What about the human?"

"Like you," she said. "Perhaps he has the Ancient genetic marker?"

He watched the little party disappear into the distance, swallowed up by the shadows cast by the vast structure ahead. "You guys know a way into this place, right?"

"Of course," Balen said. "There's always a backdoor."

In this case, the backdoor involved a long and perilous climb up a narrow stairway cut into the cliff, with nothing but the ocean waves to break your fall — before they smashed you against the rocks. Nice thought.

By the time he reached the top Jack was sweating, his skin starting to crisp in the intense sunlight. If Carter had been there, she'd have had some kind of scanner to warn them about high UV levels. But, of course, she wasn't there. None of his team was there. They were being held hostage by the creepy reptile guys.

Maybe.

Balen led them through a narrow doorway into a cramped and dark passage. It smelled musty, like damp rock, and abandoned. The rest of the outpost soared above them and Jack figured the basement was as good a place as any to start. "Now what?" he whispered as Hartkans and the rest of Balen's people crowded in behind him.

"The device is several floors up," Hartkans said. "Balen knows the way and we can —"

"Wait. Where's my team?" Not that they were really his team anymore, but still. "Where are they holding SG-1?"

"We'll find them after," Hartkans said, glancing at his watch. It glowed in the dark and Jack could see a timer counting down. "Come on, we don't have long."

"Before what?"

"Before it's too late." Hartkans fixed him with a look. "For your team."

*And you know this, how?* Jack thought, but kept it to himself. There were far too many unknowns here for his liking.

There were no lights at first, only a faint illumination filtering down the stairs from higher up. But despite the gloom, Jack could see that everything was getting increasingly fancy the further they went: swirly patterns carved into the rock, the steps opening out into a broad staircase, and eventually the lights activating as they passed.

Hartkans stopped, surprised the first time it happened.

"Motion sensor?" Jack suggested.

But Hartkans shook his head. "You did it," he said. "The outpost's responding to your ATA gene."

Jack tried not to be creeped out by the fact that this Ancient pile of stones could somehow detect his genetic code. "I should get some of these installed at home," was all he said out loud. "It would save—"

Something detonated above them. The explosion shivered through the stone stairs, followed by a concussed silence when all Jack could hear was ringing in his ears. "What—?" The clatter of falling masonry cut him off, clouds of dust billowing down the stairs and making them all cough.

"Damn it," Hartkans growled, glancing at his watch.

Balen snarled something in her own language. "You said they wouldn't be here yet."

"There's still time," Hartkans said. "Keep moving."

Jack didn't bother asking who 'they' were. He doubted Hartkans would tell him the truth, and he'd find out for himself soon enough. He unsafetied his weapon and followed as Hartkans started running up the stairs.

The noise of a firefight began to filter through the dust and he could hear energy weapons discharging—a staff blast? "Jaffa?" he called to Hartkans.

"Oranian pistol," Hartkans said, spitting dust from his mouth. He stopped when the stairs reached an intersecting corridor, glancing both ways. "Balen?"

"That way," she said, indicating left. Unsurprisingly, it was the direction from which all the shooting was coming.

"Something unexpected?" he asked Hartkans.

Hartkans' face was tight. "We have to get to that device first," he said. "Everything depends on it."

Jack didn't answer, but did notice the lack of 'sir' in the orders Hartkans was throwing around. He kept his hands on his gun, using it to gesture along the corridor. "After you, *Major*," he said.

Hartkans gave him a cold stare, then looked past him — probably at Balen. "We can't afford to screw this up."

Jack said nothing, but he could sense the weapon aimed at his back and knew he had no choice but to follow as Hartkans crept along the corridor. It was pretty clear what would happen if he didn't cooperate.

Daylight spilled into the corridor up ahead, through the shattered remains of a door that had been blown out from within. He glanced into the room and saw a long slender window and a shard of sunlight falling across the floor, glinting against something silver that lay in the dust: the wrapper from a military issue power bar.

But there was no time to comment because suddenly they were under attack.

"They're behind us!" Balen yelled and Jack spun, dropping to one knee as a streak of gunfire scorched overhead. It was some kind of energy weapon he didn't recognize. Oranian, he guessed from the fact that a group of the bastards was bearing down on them at a run.

"Hold your ground!" Hartkans yelled, and he opened up with his P90 at the same time Jack did. The enemy went down easily, but there were more behind them. Many more.

Jack edged to the side of the corridor, offering a narrower target. "We need cover!" he barked at Hartkans.

But Hartkans wasn't paying attention. "Tark," he yelled. "Get O'Neill to the device. We'll hold them here."

"What —" Jack began, but Balen grabbed his arm and hauled him to his feet. She was strong.

"Come on," she said. "We can end this now."

He hesitated, but Hartkans and the rest of Balen's people were holding the corridor, and going with Balen at least offered him options.

They ran, clambering over the rubble from the doorway, then further on into a clearer section of the corridor.

"This way," Balen said, skidding to a halt. "Shortcut."

He would have missed the narrow opening in the wall, but Balen obviously knew it was there and squeezed through. Jack followed. He doubted it was part of the original Ancient design, but the rough set of handholds cut into the rock was easy enough to climb. Above him, Balen disappeared through a hole, and a moment later his own head was poking into the room above.

Balen was already at the door, pressing her ear against it, as Jack pushed himself up through the hole and stayed crouched for a moment.

On the far side of the room sat a pedestal with something glowing and definitely Ancient on top. Cautiously, he got to his feet. "That it?" he said.

Balen nodded but didn't leave the doorway. "They're out there."

"Who are?"

"Trouble," she said.

Jack moved so that the pedestal was between himself and Balen, but kept his eyes on the device. It was a domed hexagon, with Ancient letters or numbers written on each of its segmented sides. Genes or no genes, he couldn't make any sense of it.

"Activate it," Balen said. "Do it now."

He glanced over at her. "How?"

"Just touch it," she said. "All it needs is your genetic marker."

The device looked innocuous, small — not much larger than a dinner plate. "And this will kill all the Oranians on this base."

"On the planet," Balen said, still nervous next to the door. "Now hurry."

"How many?"

Irritated, she glanced back over her shoulder. "What?"

"How many Oranians on the planet?"

"I don't know. What does it matter? They'll all be dead."

Jack cocked an eyebrow. "That's why it matters."

Balen's eyes narrowed. "They'll kill your friends."

"So you say."

She shifted, turning her back on the door now — perhaps she'd figured out the greater threat was inside the room. Jack's hands dropped to his P90.

"Activate the device," Balen said. "Kill the Oranians, or we'll all die here."

"And what happens when it's done?" He nodded toward the weapon she held loose at her side. He didn't recognize its design, but it looked lethal. "You kill me and make off with the doomsday device?"

Balen bared her teeth in what might have been a smile. "We could be allies, you and I," she said, a lascivious glint in her eye as she strolled closer. "We could do great things, O'Neill. Explore the galaxy, get rich. With this device, we could rule worlds."

"Yeah," Jack said, "I'm more of a hockey fan."

Balen's face hardened. "Activate the device," she said, her weapon coming up in one smooth motion.

"I'm gonna guess," he said, lifting his own gun, "that you need me alive to activate this thing."

"Only barely."

"Thing is," Jack said, "I don't need you alive at all."

"Well that's odd." Daniel stared at the door panel in surprise. "It's working."

"Just means there's power here," said Cam. "The lights are on too."

"Or," Daniel said, "there's someone inside that room with the ATA gene."

"Will you hurry up?" Vala hissed from a dozen yards farther down the corridor. "They're coming this way."

He didn't need her to tell him that, he could hear the gunfire. "Who do you think they're fighting?" he asked Cam.

"It is irrelevant," Teal'c said. "All that matters is destroying the device held within this room."

"Right," he said, smiling at Teal'c's patient reminder to focus.

"You guys ready?"

"For what?" said Cam.

Daniel shrugged. "For whatever's in here."

Mitchell raised his weapon, and so did Teal'c. Behind them, Vala backed closer to them, although her eyes were still turned in the direction of the firefight. "Let's just get inside," she said. "Before we have company."

Daniel pulled his Beretta from its holster, holding it low as he pressed his hand on the door activation panel. It shot open and Mitchell was through it immediately, Teal'c at his shoulder. Daniel and Vala followed, fanning out behind them, weapons raised. The door hissed shut.

"Don't move," Mitchell barked, although it didn't look like anyone was moving in the unexpected tableau before them. A woman — Lucian Alliance, by the look of her clothes — stood with her back to them, the Oranian pistol she held aimed at the head of a young, oddly familiar, US airman who had his P90 pointed right back at her.

"Welcome to the party," said the airman, without shifting his focus from the woman. "I hope you brought snacks."

It was the voice that gave him away, knocking the ground out from beneath Daniel's feet. "Jack?"

A flicker of a glance in his direction, then a flash of the same astonishment he felt. "Daniel?"

Jack's weapon wavered for a fraction of a second and the woman pounced, reaching across the pedestal to grab his vest. "Back off!" she yelled, hauling him toward her over the device as she pressed her gun to his head. "Back off, or he dies."

Jack dropped his P90, letting it hang from his tac vest, and flung his arms out wide, as far from the device as possible.

No one else moved.

"I mean it," the woman said, glaring at Daniel. "I'll kill him."

"She won't," Jack said. "She needs me to activate the device. I have some kind of gene…"

"Yeah," Daniel said. "We know."

"You want your friend to live?" the woman said. "Then leave. Now."

Cam threw Daniel a glance, deferring to his decision. Carefully, Daniel lowered his weapon. Mitchell and Teal'c did the same, but Vala was standing directly behind the woman, unobserved. "Careful," Daniel said, his words aimed at Vala although his eyes were fixed on the woman holding the gun to Jack's head. "Easy does it."

"Now back off," she said, shifting a little closer to Jack. Vala moved with her, silent as a thief.

"Just shoot her," said Jack.

"You're a fool," the woman hissed. "You're turning your back on a fortune."

"Really? I thought we were here to avenge the deaths of your people."

She grinned, showing wide teeth. "What better way to avenge them than by stealing the most valuable weapon in the galaxy from under the noses of the Oranians?"

"Huh," Jack said. "Oranians have noses?"

Daniel almost grinned, touched by bittersweet nostalgia despite the precarious situation — or, perhaps, because of it. He glanced past the woman's shoulder, caught Vala's eye. It was time. The woman must have seen the look because she half turned, but not before Vala's well-placed shot sent her twitching to the floor in a haze of blue energy.

Released, Jack backed away, watching them all with a mixture of doubt and suspicion. Daniel didn't miss the tense hold he had on his weapon.

"Daniel," Vala said, lowering her zat. "What's going on? Who is this guy?"

"I'm Jack O'Neill," Jack said. "Who the hell are you?"

He'd recognized the cold sweep of Asgard transporter technology the moment the beam touched him, dissolving his mind and reforming it someplace else.

Not an Asgard ship, though. Human. *Prometheus*?

He was in what they'd called 'guest quarters' but, despite the soft furnishings and the decent meal they'd provided, the airman stationed outside his door gave the lie to the term 'guest'.

He'd been there several hours. Time enough for the others to mop up the mess on the planet and to put the Ancient weapon permanently beyond use. They were in motion now, travelling faster than light back to Earth, and probably trying to figure out what the hell to do with an extra Jack O'Neill.

Lying on the bed, hands behind his head, he stared out at the blurred star field and wondered whether he should have made a break for it back on the planet. Once he'd reached the Stargate he could have gone anywhere, could have been free. But free to do what? His life had always been about service, and, without that, what meaning would there be in wandering the galaxy? But the thought of returning to his life on Earth, of knowing that incredible things were happening beyond his reach, was profoundly depressing. It was almost enough to make him wish he'd taken Balen Tark up on her offer.

When the door to his quarters eventually opened, he wasn't surprised to see Daniel and Teal'c standing outside. They looked different from how he remembered them — older, changed by experiences he hadn't shared — but they were still the same men. To him, they looked like old friends. Whether they were or not remained to be seen.

He sat up and swung his legs over the side of the bed, but didn't stand as they entered. Teal'c nodded to the airman and the door slid shut, leaving them alone together.

"So," Daniel said after a short silence, "this is a mess."

"I'm guessing," Jack said, "there is no Major Hartkans?"

"Nope." Daniel moved further into the room and took a seat in one of the chairs next to the small desk in the corner. Teal'c remained standing near the door, hands behind his back. He looked odd with hair, the lines on his face more profound, but he still looked like Teal'c.

"Hartkans," Daniel said, "is ex-NID, a former member of a shadow organization called The Trust. Now it looks like he's working with the Lucian Alliance. Balen Tark is one of the new leaders that emerged after their failed attack on Earth."

"And what's the Lucian Alliance?"

"A loose coalition of smugglers, arms dealers and thieves," Teal'c said. "They have grown to prominence in the power vacuum created by the destruction of the Goa'uld."

Jack glanced at Daniel for confirmation. "So that's true, then?" he said. "Turner fed me a lot of crap. I didn't know how much to believe."

"It's true," Daniel said, "the System Lords are gone." He let a beat fall. "Including Ba'al, by the way. He was executed by the Tok'ra. I saw him die."

"Good," was all he said, because ten years on he still had nightmares and he didn't see them ending just because Ba'al was gone. He pushed a hand through his hair, as if he could scrub away the memories.

"And the Jaffa are free," Teal'c added, with restrained but deep pride.

Jack smiled, though he felt a weight of sadness. "I wish I could have been there to see that."

"You know why you couldn't," Daniel said. "You know why you shouldn't be here now."

"Paperwork?"

"Something like that."

A long beat fell. "So now what?"

"Now you go home." A frown creased Daniel's forehead, the furrows cutting a little deeper than of old. "Colonel Caldwell wanted to beam you to the SGC for a full debrief, but Cam and I convinced him it wasn't necessary."

"I don't know," Jack said. "I wouldn't mind seeing the old place again."

"The brig?"

"Even that."

"Jack…"

"You have no idea!" he snapped. "To know all this is out here and to have no one — *no one* — to talk to about it? No way to help. To be cut off from everything and everyone that matters?" He dropped his head into his hands, trying to keep a lid on it all. "You have no idea, Daniel."

There was a long silence, Daniel for once apparently lost for words.

It was Teal'c who spoke in the end. "There are many things that matter, O'Neill," he said. "Not all of them are to be found beyond the Stargate."

"There's nothing that matters more than this," Jack said, looking up. "And you know it."

Teal'c lifted an eyebrow. "You were willing to die for the Tau'ri," he said. "Is Earth so perfect that there is no cause there worthy of the same sacrifice?"

"It's different," Jack said. "Out here —"

"There is great evil in your world, O'Neill. I have seen it. There is war, there is suffering, and there are men as cruel and corrupt as any System Lord. Why do you not oppose them?"

"Hey," he objected, "I can't even join the military — I'm barred, remember? And what else can I do? I'm just one man."

"As was I, when first I opposed the Goa'uld." He fixed Jack with a look. "There is always a way to fight for the people of your world, O'Neill."

Daniel gave him a sideways look. "Um, Teal'c? I'm not sure that's such a good idea."

"Why not, Daniel Jackson? O'Neill is a man of great skill and ingenuity. This cloned body he now possesses gives him youthful vitality to complement his experience and wisdom." His attention returned to Jack. "You could make a difference to your planet."

"He could get himself killed."

Jack felt his heartbeat kick up a notch. Maybe Teal'c was

right. Maybe he'd been so fixated on what he couldn't do out here that he hadn't considered what he could do closer to home. Iraq, Syria, Somalia, a dozen other hotspots around the world — could he somehow make a difference? Could he help make Earth a planet worth dying to protect? "Well, it's a thought," he said and watched the smile twitch the corner of Teal'c's mouth.

A stomach-lurching shift in the ship's motion made Daniel glance up at the ceiling. "We've dropped out of hyperspace."

"Home already?"

Daniel just nodded to the window behind Jack's head. He turned, standing slowly, breath catching as it always did at the sight of the beautiful blue planet.

"Home," said Daniel.

Jack moved to the window, pressed a hand against the glass. This would probably be the last time he ever saw this sight, ever left the confines of the world below. It was the end. "I miss you all," he said, without looking around. "I miss the SGC. I miss my life." He took a breath, blew it out slowly. "But you don't miss me. Jack O'Neill is still in your lives. And I'm not him."

Neither of them tried to deny it, but he heard Daniel get to his feet and come to stand by his side at the window. "I'm sorry," he said after a while. "It must be very difficult."

Jack just nodded. "Hartkans told me George Hammond died."

"Yeah," Daniel said with a catch in his voice. "A couple of years ago."

"I wish I'd known. I'd have liked to pay my respects." He hesitated before he spoke again, bracing himself for the answer. "What about Carter? She's not with SG-1 anymore?"

"She's okay," Daniel assured him. "She's Colonel Carter now, commanding the *George Hammond*. That's a ship," he added, as if Jack couldn't guess. "Like this one, only better."

Relieved, proud, and a dozen other things he tried not to feel when it came to Carter, he said, "Well, that's pretty cool."

"Yeah." Daniel cleared his throat. "Listen, um, you should probably know that she and Jack are —"

"Don't," he said, cutting him off. "I don't want to know."

Daniel nodded and after a moment said, "And that's why you can't stay. You can't be a ghost in your own life."

"I know that."

"It's tough, but — God, look at you. You're young, you're strong. Don't waste time looking back."

Jack swallowed a retort and turned away from the window. Daniel, older now than Jack was, regarded him with serious eyes. Teal'c, strange with his white-streaked hair, stood watching him from the door. Good men, good friends — but not *his* friends. He had to let them go, for real this time.

He glanced up at the ceiling. They'd beamed him right into these quarters, he figured they could beam him right out again. "So I just click my heels and say 'There's no place like home'?"

Daniel smiled. "When you're ready."

He took a breath. "I'm ready."

"Then take care of yourself, Jack. Stay out of trouble."

"You too."

Daniel tapped something in his ear and said, "Ready to transport in five, four…"

But before the beam activated, Teal'c crossed the room. With a rebellious look at Daniel he said, "Do *not* stay out of trouble, O'Neill. Seek trouble out." He unholstered his zat, handed it to him. "And when you find it, fix it."

Jack turned the gun over in his hands, a slow grin spreading across his face. "You betcha," he said as the Asgard beam swept him away.

Dawn was breaking over the mountains when Jack materialized in the parking lot of Bosco's Tavern, still wearing his BDUs and holding Teal'c's zat in his hands. The air was cool, fresh with promise, and he let it fill his lungs. Eyes closed, he lifted his face to the sun and for a moment he simply existed — young and strong, with life rolling out ahead of him.

A breeze ruffled his hair and he opened his eyes. It was time to begin.

Jogging over to his bike, he dug the keys out of his tac vest before shrugging it off and stuffing it and the zat into the top box. He'd just fired up the engine when an old man with a broom came out from behind the tavern, sweeping early fall leaves.

He nodded when he saw Jack. "We don't open for breakfast 'til six-thirty."

"That's okay," Jack said. "I'm not staying."

Leaning on the broom, the guy looked at him the way old men look at the young — a mixture of envy and indulgence. "And where're you headed so early, son?"

Jack grinned. "Trouble, sir," he said and gunned the engine, turning the bike toward the road and the sunrise. "I'm headed for trouble."

# CHAPTER ONE

THE THIRD time he woke, it was to a cacophony of noise—chatter in a language he only half understood. There was pain all over, but most acute in his ribs and face. It was a familiar pain, though: broken bones, bruised tissue, and sliced skin. He knew how to handle it.

With some effort, he opened his eyes. Well, one eye. The other wasn't cooperating and he could feel the swelling even though he couldn't lift his bound hands to touch his face. Through his one good eye he saw a world canted sideways: the interior of a bombed-out shell of a building, young men in a semblance of military dress with Kalashnikovs to hand.

A bead of sweat ran down his forehead, into his eye. It was hot in the room, stifling, and the bright streak of light slicing through the shattered window told him it was still morning. He figured he'd only been out for a few moments.

He was tempted to drift off again, but it was already too late. Someone had noticed he was awake. The guy—little more than a kid, really—nudged his colleague and both of them turned around, exchanging a few words.

And then it began again: the shouting, the beating, the smart phone shoved in his face to capture it all. Consciousness ebbed and flowed, mind detaching and swimming into memories, into nightmares. And at last, because everyone does in the end, he started to talk. "Colonel… Colonel Jack O'Neill." The words slurred around the blood in his mouth. "US Air Force. Serial number 799-36-6412."

It was a relief when the zat sent him convulsing into oblivion. He kinda hoped they'd shoot him a second time.

General Hank Landry leaned back in his seat as he regarded the people looking back at him across his desk. "I'm truly sorry for your situation," he said, treading carefully, "but what you're asking is … difficult, to say the least."

"We appreciate that, General Landry." Teyla Emagan sat very still, fingers laced on the table in front of her. Hank didn't know her well, but he'd warmed to her frank and open expression. "We would not ask if the situation were not dire."

"Sheppard's going to die." Ronon Dex was far less diplomatic than his colleague. "Unless we can find a way to get that Ancient data out of his head, he's going to die."

Landry took a breath and met the man's fierce glare. "I understand that, but you're asking the Head of Homeworld Command to risk his life to save him. That's no small ask."

A rap on the door interrupted them, followed by Daniel Jackson's head poking around the doorframe. "Ah, sorry, you wanted to see me, General?"

"Yes," Landry said, and tried not to consider Jackson as backup. "Come in. You know Teyla and Ronon, I think."

"Of course." Jackson had a smile for their guests. "How are you?"

"Unfortunately," Teyla said, "we're here on a matter of great urgency. " She glanced at Landry for permission to continue and he nodded. "On a recent mission, Colonel Sheppard encountered an Ancient Repository of knowledge. We had not realized it was operational until it was too late …"

She trailed off and Jackson winced. "It downloaded the library of Ancient knowledge into his brain?"

"Yes. That was three days ago. We know we do not have long to find a way to remove it before Colonel Sheppard's mind is effected, but without the assistance of the Asgard it is difficult."

Jackson pulled up a third chair and sat down, angled forward in concern. "Did you try contacting the Vanir?"

"Yes, but without success."

Jackson shared a helpless look with Landry. "I'm not sure how much help we can be," he said. "The two times it happened to Jack, it was the Asgard who helped him."

"That is why we're here." Teyla's gaze left Jackson and returned to Hank.

He said, "They want to use Jack O'Neill's mind as a—map, of sorts."

Jackson's eyebrows rose, brow crinkling. "A map?"

"It's a crude metaphor," Teyla confessed, sounding frustrated, "but essentially Rodney and Dr. Beckett hope that there may be some residue, some formatting, if you like, in General O'Neill's mind that they can use to help find a way to reprogram the device to remove the data from John's mind." She paused. "There must be some trace left behind, some clue."

"So you need some sort of brain scan?" Jackson asked. "I'm sure Jack would be willing to help, but—"

"Not a brain scan," Landry said. "They'd need O'Neill to travel to M67-2Y5 and connect to the Ancient Repository device himself. If it works, McKay will be able to use the residue code in O'Neill's brain to reprogram the repository and upload the information back out of Sheppard's mind."

"And if it doesn't?"

"It would download it into O'Neill's mind. And we'd have lost two good men, instead of one."

Jackson's jaw tightened. "That's …" He ran a hand through his hair. "The thing is, even if Jack was willing, which, knowing Jack he would be, the IOA and the Joint Chiefs … they'd never permit it. Jack's just too important to the whole Stargate program."

"So's Sheppard," Ronon said, angry and bullish. "Without O'Neill's help, he *will* die. There's no maybe about *that*."

Teyla reached out and put a quelling hand on his arm. "We ask you to at least put the question to General O'Neill. We will take every step to ensure his safety." Her glance flicked sideways at Ronon, but she appeared to ignore his slight headshake. "Even though M67-2Y5 is within Wraith territory."

Landry chewed on that, exchanging another weighted look

with Jackson. They both knew what Jack would want to do, with or without the approval of the IOA, and neither wanted to put that weight on his shoulders.

"I guess he needs to know," Jackson said, with a barely concealed sigh.

"But the warning stands," Hank said, "that the decision may not be his."

Teyla nodded, her hand still resting on Ronon's arm. "Thank you, General. We understand."

And perhaps she did, but Ronon's glower said something very different.

Landry rose to his feet, ending the meeting, the others following suit. "I'll keep you posted on our progress," he told them, moving around his desk toward the door to the briefing room. "I understand that Colonel Sheppard's time is limited, so I'll ensure this receives urgent attention. In the meantime, if there's anything Dr. Lam can do to assist Dr. Beckett, please ask him to contact us immediately."

"Thank you," Teyla said, with a gracious nod to them both and then, with a look at Ronon, they both left, crossing the briefing room toward the stairs to the control room.

Jackson made to follow, but Landry held him back with a touch on his arm. "You know Jack won't be able to go," he said in a low voice. "It's impossible."

"Yeah," Jackson agreed. "So I guess we'll have to find another solution."

"Is there one?"

Jackson didn't bother to reply to that; the bleak expression on his face was answer enough.

As far as General O'Neill was concerned, it was a normal day at the Pentagon.

He stopped for coffee and a donut on his way in and still hit his desk by eight o'clock. He worked through his email with his finger on the delete button, ran through his diary with his assistant, and only occasionally glanced up at the ceiling to wonder whether the *Hammond* had left orbit yet. He'd said his goodbyes to Sam the previous day, but still—Pegasus was a galaxy far, far away and not a particularly safe one either. It helped to stay busy.

Just as he was gathering his crap together for the day's first meeting, the phone rang. And he'd have let it go to voicemail if the caller ID hadn't said 'Janet Napolitano'. His eyebrows rose, a pulse of unease thrumming low in his gut. It wasn't every day the Secretary of Homeland Security called him personally. In fact, it wasn't any day.

He was still on his feet when he took the call. "General O'Neill."

"General," Napolitano said. "My office is sending you a video over secure channels. It was posted online two hours ago. We've taken steps to have it removed, but I need you to watch it and call me right back."

He barely had time for a "Yes ma'am" before the line went dead. "Okay," he said to the empty office, still holding the phone. "That's ... odd."

The email was already there when he refreshed his in-box. He hit play, sitting back in his chair to watch. A nasty but familiar scene unfolded: a western hostage having the crap beaten out of him somewhere in the Middle East. Been there, done that, he thought sourly, but didn't understand what this poor bastard had to do with either him or the Stargate program.

The guy's face was swollen and disfigured, the shaky smart phone image dancing about and making it difficult to decipher detail. But then the focus zoomed in on the guy and something cold ran the length of Jack's spine. He sat up, leaning forward toward the screen. What the hell...?

The guy's lips were moving, like he was trying to talk. "Colonel..." he managed at first. Then, "Colonel Jack O'Neill..." He spat out a mouthful of blood, barely conscious. "US Air Force. Serial number 799-36-6412."

General O'Neill just stared at the screen, dumbfounded.

And then there was another face in front of the camera, mostly hidden behind a scarf, but the words he spoke were clear enough. "We have your spy," the man said in accented English, and held up something that made O'Neill catch his breath. "And we have your weapon—we'll find more."

Turning around, the guy aimed the zat at the prisoner and fired.

The screen went blank and O'Neill stared at it for a moment, mind spinning through all the possibilities and coming up blank. What the hell had he just seen? What in—?

He snatched up the phone, punched the speed dial to the SGC and waited with zero patience. Luckily, the call was picked up right away. "Jack, I was just about to call—"

"Is the *Hammond* still in orbit?"

Landry paused for a beat. "She's finalizing system checks now. Is there a problem?"

"Yeah. I need Carter to report to my office. Now. Daniel too, if he's around."

Another beat of silence came down the line before Landry said, "I take it you're not expecting them to fly in from Peterson?"

"I mean *now*, Hank."

"Understood. Standby."

O'Neill hung up the phone, poked his head out the door and told his assistant to cancel all his morning meetings. "And no one comes in or out," he added.

"Yes sir." Lieutenant Liu had been working for him long enough not to ask any stupid questions.

Nonetheless, O'Neill pulled down the blinds on his office window just to be sure and moved back around his desk to wait. It felt like one of the longest five minutes he'd endured, just staring at the frozen image on his screen, but at last the transporter flared white and deposited a somewhat irritated looking Colonel Carter and a bemused Daniel Jackson in the middle of his office.

"General," Carter said, not doing a great job of hiding her frustration. "We're twenty minutes from departure…"

Daniel scrubbed a hand through his hair. "I'm assuming this is actually a matter of life or death," he said, "and nothing to do with you not being able to finish the crossword?"

O'Neill ignored them both and swiveled his monitor around. "Watch."

They watched.

In other circumstances, it might have been funny to see the way Carter's eyes went round as saucers, or the way Daniel's jaw dropped. As it was, O'Neill mostly felt a headache building behind his eyes and when the video cut out he looked over at them and said, "Well?"

Carter blinked, shaking her head, but Daniel looked distinctly shifty. "Um," he said, rubbing at the back of his neck, "so I guess that's mini-me? As in, mini-*you*."

"The clone?" Carter glanced back at the frozen image on the screen. "He's in…? Where is that, Iraq?"

"Or somewhere," O'Neill said, his patience slipping. "Apparently he's in the Middle East with a freakin' *zat!*"

"Ah," Daniel said with a wince that made O'Neill's stomach sink.

"*Ah?*" He narrowed his eyes and grabbed hold of his patience with both hands. "Daniel, tell me you don't know anything about this."

Daniel sighed, pulled off his glasses and said, "Not exactly."

"Not *exactly*?"

"Look, okay— Teal'c and I may have run into 'Jonathan O'Neill' off-world last year."

"You—?" Jack didn't often do speechless—he'd seen almost everything there was to see in his long career—but for this he was making an exception and all he could do was echo Daniel's words. "You ran into him *off-world*?"

Daniel at least had the good grace to look uncomfortable.

"He'd been recruited by the Trust. It was a sensitive situation, I didn't want—"

"You ran into him off-world and I haven't read about it in *one single* report?"

"Look," Daniel said, fixing him with that oh-so-familiar rebellious glare. "What happened wasn't his fault, but I knew you'd have to escalate it if you found out. And I knew what the IOA would do to him." He folded his arms across his chest, chin lifted. "I couldn't let that happen. Cam agreed."

"He's meant to be staying the hell away from the Stargate Program," O'Neill barked. "That was the deal!"

Daniel's expression tightened further. "He's you, Jack. He's you without..." He waved his hand around the office and in the general direction of Sam. "...without *anything*. He was cut off from everything and everyone he knew and it was driving him nuts, okay? He was in a bad way, and we— Well, Teal'c and I suggested that maybe there were battles he could fight at home as well as off-world. A way he could use his, uh, talents." His gaze returned to the screen. "Looks like he found one."

Carter let a breath out, hissing through her teeth. "Daniel..."

"You didn't meet him," he said quietly. "Sam, he was— Look, okay, maybe the zat was a bad idea."

"Ya think?" O'Neill growled.

"But he needed something," Daniel insisted. "Jack, come on, you have to understand that; he's *you*."

"He's *not* me," O'Neill snapped. "He's— Look, I don't know what he is, but right now he's a problem. A loose end we need to tie up." He pointed at the phone. "The Secretary of Homeland Security is waiting for my call right now. And I have no idea what to tell her."

Silence for a moment, then Carter said, "Do we know exactly where he is?"

"We know exactly what's in that video."

"The interrogator's dialect is Syrian," Daniel offered. "Levantine Arabic—maybe from Homs, by the inflection."

"The *Hammond* could run a scan," Carter suggested. She threw O'Neill a wry glance. "At least we have his DNA and I should be able to configure our scanners to look for it. Then you could send in an extraction team."

O'Neill pinched the bridge of his nose, trying to imagine how the conversation would go with the Joint Chiefs. "We don't have boots on the ground in Syria," he said, "and the last thing we need is a Special Ops team coming face-to-face with that zat and going home talking about ray guns."

"Well..." She lifted her eyebrows. "I could send a team from the *Hammond*, beam them straight in and out again, with, uh, with the clone."

Now that...? That sounded like a plan. Not an entirely legal one, but it wouldn't be the first time he'd bent the rules in the name of expediency. He fixed Carter with a steady look to make sure she understood the consequences of what she was proposing. "We'd have to fly below the radar."

"Actually above it," she said with a slight smile. "But, yes."

The repercussions of a foul up didn't bear thinking about, but they'd certainly end his career. Carter's too. But his eyes dipped to the image on the screen and, no matter how much he wanted to deny it, Daniel's assertion that the guy was *him* was difficult to deny. At the very least he was his responsibility. Besides, O'Neill didn't leave people behind enemy lines.

Into the silence that had fallen he said, "How long do you need?"

"Half a day to calibrate the scanners, another half day to run the scan. Let's call it twenty-four hours before we can send in a team."

O'Neill gave the nod. "Do it."

"What will you do with him?" Daniel said, his attention still on the screen. "Lock him up?"

O'Neill ran a hand through his hair, let out a slow breath. "I have no idea, Daniel. Not a single one."

For obvious reasons, the existence of the cloned O'Neill had been kept a closely guarded secret ever since Loki had brought him into existence. Mostly, that had been for his own protection and at Jack's—the real Jack's—insistence. He'd thought the guy deserved a shot at a real life, but to Sam it had always seemed impossible that 'Jonathan O'Neill' could simply wipe more than twenty years of life and military experience from his mind and start over. If the decision had made Sam uncomfortable then, now it left her feeling horribly guilty. Of course he could never adapt to that new vanilla life. Of course something like this would happen.

The sight of him tied up and beaten had shocked her, twisting a familiar fear tight in the pit of her stomach. It didn't help that he looked so much more like the Jack she knew than the kid they'd met all those years ago. But worse than that was the thought of how he'd gotten there. The idea of him just packing his bags and heading into a war zone to try and do some good, while she and the rest of the SGC carried on with their lives, made her want to hit something. How could they have let that happen? How could they have left him out there alone?

When she thought about it now, it was almost too painful to imagine what it must have been like for him to lose everything: his friends, his career, his home, and his past, not to mention all his possessions, every memento of his life. How could a man move beyond that? How could a man re-forge his life when everything that made him who he was had been stripped away?

The fact that it was Jack O'Neill only made it worse, because she *knew* him—and she knew exactly how impossible it would have been for him to break those ties. The thought filled her with an intense guilt, not least because she *hadn't* spent the past eleven years thinking about this other version of Jack

O'Neill. She was ashamed to admit it, but he'd slipped her mind. Amid all of the world-saving SG-1 had been called upon to do, she hadn't thought about this other Jack struggling on alone out there. And maybe no one would blame her for that, but Sam still felt like, somehow, she'd let him down. Like she'd left him behind. And that was something she'd vowed to never ever do.

Shaking off the thoughts, she refocused on the task at hand. Engineering was quiet because it was late and only the night crew was on duty. She could have had someone else monitor the sensor sweep, but doing it herself helped her deal with her guilt. As she so often had in the past, she felt a driving need to fix the problem herself—to ensure that the sensors were correctly recalibrated, to painstakingly scan the region, to pull O'Neill out of enemy hands.

If he was still alive.

The thought made her shiver and she reached for the dregs of her coffee and tried to swallow the idea down. No point in dwelling on what she couldn't change; it only diverted her attention away from what she could.

"Sam?" Daniel's quiet voice came from the doorway where he stood, coffee in hand. "Any luck?"

She shook her head, stretched her back a little. "Not yet, but it's only a matter of time. Finding one guy, one unique DNA sequence, amid a couple million people..."

"The proverbial needle in a haystack," he said as he walked into the room and took a seat. "Thanks for having me aboard, by the way." He lifted his coffee in a kind of salute. "It would have been a long wait at the SGC."

"No problem."

"I feel kinda—" He frowned, brows knitting above his glasses. "Responsible, I guess. I feel like, I don't know, like..."

"Like we abandoned him?"

Daniel nodded. "When we saw him last year, Sam, he was— He looked so much like Jack, and yet so... I don't know, so lost

I guess. Desperate, in a way."

She squeezed her eyes closed against that image. "We didn't exactly handle it well," she sighed. "The whole clone thing."

"But what else could we have done? It was his best shot at rebuilding a life."

There was no real answer to that; it was impossible to know how things might have turned out if he'd stayed in the Stargate Program. And wouldn't it have been equally difficult for there to be two Jack O'Neills trying to inhabit the same life? On a personal level it would have been, well, impossible. She ran a hand through her hair and stifled a yawn. It was late and she was about to ask Daniel if he'd get her something to eat when a quiet alert sounded from the scanner.

She sat up straight. "Oh," she said, toggling the alert off. "Here we go..."

Daniel was at her shoulder immediately, leaning in. "Is it him?"

"Possibly. Showing a ninety-six percent DNA match... ninety-eight percent." She watched the numbers shift, anticipation warring with unease. And then, "Bingo," she said and glanced up with a smile. "It's him."

"Alive?"

She shook her head. "Can't tell, it's just a DNA match."

Daniel took a moment to process that, then said, "So where is he?"

She brought up the map, zoomed in. "Well, you were right about Syria," she said. "He's about three klicks north of Raqqa— Al-Nusra territory."

"Okay, nice," Daniel said with exactly as much dread as she felt.

Pushing herself her feet, she headed for the door. "I need to contact General O'Neill, get my team ready—"

"Sam?"

She stopped, looking back. "Daniel, if you're going to tell me I shouldn't lead the mission myself, you can forget—"

"I was going to ask if you've got room for one more on the team."

"Daniel..."

"I speak Arabic," he pointed out, watching her over the tops of his glasses. "And I'm pretty handy with a gun, you know."

And, Sam figured, if she felt the need to assuage her guilt by going back for 'Jack' herself, then why would Daniel feel any different? She offered him a wry smile, already imagining the general's objections, and said, "Go gear up, we're leaving in an hour."

Jack was in the ruins of what once, maybe, had been a home or a shop. The floor was concrete, the windows blown out but secured by bars. He probably couldn't have gotten past them even if his arms weren't tied behind his back.

It was dark out now, the night bringing some relief from the heat, although the chill wasn't a whole lot better. At least he'd stopped sweating. With some effort, Jack pushed himself into a sitting position, propping one shoulder against the wall and giving his spinning head time to adjust. His face was throbbing, one eye still swollen shut, and he figured he'd lost enough blood to explain the wooziness. Not to mention the fact that he couldn't remember the last time he'd eaten.

There was gunfire in the distance, a couple shells landing several klicks away, and from directly outside the building drifted the quiet chatter of whoever was guarding this place. Kids, mostly, from what he could tell.

He had no idea what had happened to the hostages he'd come here to free, but he hoped they were still running. Last thing he'd seen before the bastards got him was the two guys piling into the waiting car and it taking off under a hail of gunfire. He hoped they'd made it out. That would at least give some meaning to the rest of this crap.

It wasn't like this was the first time he'd been captured behind enemy lines, of course, but it was the first time he'd been a *civilian* captured behind enemy lines. Not that these goons knew that. They thought he was 'Colonel Jack O'Neill' and imagined that the Air Force still gave a rat's ass about what happened to him. More fool them. Truth was that no one was coming for him. No one even knew he was here. "Joke's on you, pal," he said out loud—or tried to say. His jaw was stiff, mouth dry, and it came out as little more than a rasp.

Still, he'd gotten out of worse before, right?

Right.

Although back then, in Iraq, he'd had reason to fight. He'd had Sara and Charlie. But now…?

With a grunt, he pushed the thought aside. He wasn't going to die here, if for no other reason than he wouldn't give these bastards the satisfaction. Growling against the pain in his arms, he pushed himself up onto his knees and from there to his feet. His legs weren't bound, which was a small mercy, and they hadn't even chained him to the wall. Rookie mistake. But then these were just kids playing with guns, tweeting their goddamn kills like it was all a freakin' game. He wondered, if they lived that long, what they'd think about it all in forty years' time. He wondered how they'd sleep at night.

Shuffling over to the window, Jack peered out across the devastated city. There was fire in the distance: buildings burning, lives lost, families shattered. All the usual casualties of war. It was a profoundly depressing sight.

Suddenly, from behind him, white light flared through the gap beneath the locked door and illuminated the whole room for a microsecond. A flashbang? Except, no bang. Whatever it was it was probably bad and he backed up against the wall. Waiting.

He hated this, being so helpless.

And then there was gunfire. Not distant this time, but right inside the building. "Crap," he hissed, but there was nothing he could do but crouch down and make a smaller target of himself. "Crap."

There were a couple of options for what was going down, neither of which he liked. Either this was an assault by government forces, or by some rival rebel faction. He doubted he'd fare well in either scenario.

Boots on the stairs and then someone yelled in English. "Colonel, over here."

The voice was *American*. Sonofabitch. "Hey!" he called, pushing back to his feet. "Hey, in here!"

But then there was more gunfire—and the sizzle of the goddamn zat they'd taken from him. "Man down!" someone yelled, and someone else started speaking fast and low in Arabic, like they were trying to talk someone down from a ledge.

Damn it, what the hell was going on?

"Stand back from the door!" another voice yelled. And then, "Fire in the hole!"

Jack flinched away, turning his back as the door blew inward. But it was only a small room and something heavy hit him on the back of the head, knocking him forward and into the wall. His knees buckled, he slumped to the floor.

And then there were hands on him, easing him up. "Jack?" a man said.

Woozy, he struggled to focus through his one good eye. "Daniel?"

"Hey," the blurry man said. "Hang in there."

Then someone else loomed in front of him, face darkened by camouflage paint and blood, a shock of blonde hair sticking out from under her watch cap.

"Carter to the *Hammond*. Get us out of here, now."

And then everything was white and bright and falling apart.

# CHAPTER TWO

SAM WINCED as Dr. Grimsby put the last Steri-strip in place over the wound above her eye. All things considered, she'd gotten off light. Major Callaghan had taken a bullet in the leg, but it wasn't life-altering. And the rest of the team was more-or-less unscathed.

"I want to see you tomorrow morning, Colonel," Grimsby said. "Or earlier if you have any headaches, nausea—you know the drill."

"Yep," she said and slid down from the bed in the *Hammond's* infirmary. "Thanks, doc."

"And rest up," he said. "You have a minor concussion, Colonel. Take it seriously."

She just smiled and patted him on the shoulder.

"I'll see that she does," came a voice from behind them and Sam turned, surprised.

"General."

O'Neill gave a tight smile, gaze lingering for a moment on the wound on her head. "Colonel. You owe me a sit-rep."

"Yes sir," she said, and followed him out of the infirmary and into the corridor, heading for the bridge. When they were alone, or as alone as possible in a ship the size of the *Hammond*, she said, "What are you doing here?"

"Pacing, mostly." He threw her a pointed look. "You led the mission yourself."

"Yes sir."

"Did I authorize that?"

Sam decided not to answer that directly. "I chose the best team for the job, sir."

"Right," he said with a look that told her he'd be returning to the topic later. Meanwhile, "You get everything you went in for?"

Sam nodded. "Your, uh, clone was transported direct to the SGC along with Daniel and the missing zat."

"Good." He cleared his throat, and more quietly said, "How was he?"

"Pretty beat up. I—I think he recognized Daniel but no one else."

He grunted a response to that and they walked on in silence.

When she glanced over at him, Sam could see he was deep in thought and after a couple more moments he said, "What about evidence?" It sounded like the words were distasteful to him, and Sam understood why. Jack O'Neill could be ruthless when necessary, but he didn't kill for the sake of convenience.

"No casualties," she told him, "but we got all their smart phones and laptops. If they want to tweet about how the US government has transporter beams and phasers they can go ahead, but it's not going to do their credibility much good."

He huffed a short laugh at that. "Okay," he said, like it was a decision, and drew to a halt outside the doors to the bridge. Letting out a slow breath, he glanced down the empty corridor each way, and for a moment General O'Neill disappeared and he was just Jack. "So heading out now, huh?"

"In a half hour." A silent moment passed between them. She hated goodbyes and they'd already done this once. "How about you? Back to DC?"

"Yup. I have a hot date with the IOA." He grimaced. "They're going to want us to stamp on this hard."

Sam nodded. "Any idea what you're going to tell them?"

"Zip." He sighed. "You got anything?"

"Sorry, but if I think of something I'll email…"

He gave a slight smile at that and then straightened his shoulders like he was bracing himself, which, she knew, he was. "Okay," he said. "So—happy trails to Pegasus, Carter."

"Thanks. I'll see you in a couple weeks."

For a moment neither of them moved, and then he lifted

his hand to lightly touch the suture on her forehead. "You take care of yourself, okay?"

She offered him a reassuring smile. "Always."

It was the smell that convinced him it was real. The mix of recycled air and cold concrete, overlaid by the faint sizzle of static and ozone, could only be Stargate Command.

He'd had vivid dreams of returning to this place ever since the day he'd walked out, but he didn't think he'd ever dreamed about the smell before. Nonetheless, he was afraid to open his eyes just in case he found himself elsewhere—back in Raqqa, maybe, or back in his empty apartment in Salida. But then he heard footsteps approaching, light and purposeful, and felt a hand on his arm. "Jack?" a woman said. "Open your eyes for me."

He tried, but they felt leaden and he couldn't move them.

"That's it," the woman said, "a little more."

He tried again, just a crack, but the light was too bright and he let his heavy lids drop as something started to pound at the base of the skull. He groaned and it must have been enough to get his message across because the lights dimmed.

"Better?"

His eyes squinted open again and an unfamiliar face swam into view. "Hey," the woman said, with a smile. "I'm Dr. Lam."

Working a little moisture into his mouth he managed to say, "Where...?"

"The infirmary. You're safe, Jack. You're at the SGC."

And with that something unfolded in the center of his chest, something he'd been holding shut for years. He wanted to ask how—how they'd found him, how they'd gotten him out—but his mind was still sluggish and he couldn't form the words properly.

"It's okay." Dr. Lam squeezed his arm. "You need to rest.

There'll be time for questions later."

Jack let his eyes shut and tried not to think *I'm home*.

There were few places on Earth—or off-world—that General O'Neill hated more than sitting before the IOA committee giving them bad news.

The new chair, who'd only been in place for three months, fixed him with a steady look. "Frankly," Mrs. Dixon-Smythe said, "I find it difficult to understand why he wasn't kept under surveillance the whole time. What were you thinking, just letting him leave Stargate Command like that?"

Schooling his features, O'Neill said, "We had no legal grounds to hold him. He hadn't committed any crime and didn't pose any threat."

"He's a *clone*," Dixon-Smythe said. "That should have been enough."

"For what? Indefinite detention without trial? He has rights."

"Rights? He's not a ... a citizen," she replied. "He's not even a real person. It's nonsense to ascribe him rights. And, as events have proven, he is a grave threat to our national security. Potentially, to the security of this planet."

O'Neill cleared his throat. "And now he's contained."

Chapman, the British representative, cleared his throat. "I'd like to know what progress has been made to discover how he came to be armed with a zat—" He glanced down at his papers to check the pronunciation. "Zat'nik'a'tel."

"He's still recovering from the beatings he received." O'Neill glided smoothly over that question. "Once the doc says it's okay, we'll debrief him." He offered a flat smile. "I'll do that myself, Mr. Chapman."

"You don't think you're too close to this, General?" Chapman tilted his head. "He is, after all, your clone."

"I think that makes me exactly the right person for the job, sir."

Dixon-Smythe shook her head. "Your judgement was flawed initially, when you allowed him to leave the oversight of the Stargate program."

"All due respect," O'Neill said, switching his gaze back to her, "that decision was General Hammond's."

"Yes," she said, "and we all know how impartial he was when it came to you, General."

It was an effort of will not to ball his hands into fists, but O'Neill felt his jaw tighten as he said, "Brigadier General Hammond was one of our greatest leaders, ma'am. And, yes, he was a personal friend, but without him the world we know would no longer exist. You should remember that."

Dixon-Smythe's lips tightened, but the uncomfortable shuffle of the other committee members held her silent.

"Obviously," Chapman said, into the tense pause, "you have a plan for how to handle the clone, going forward?"

"My people are working on it," O'Neill said, "but until we've had time to debrief him—"

"Let's get one thing straight from the outset," Dixon-Smythe said. "The clone is not to be released. We simply can't risk a repeat of this. Or worse. Do you understand?"

O'Neill cast his eyes around the rest of the committee, but there were no dissenters. And, reluctantly, he had to include himself in that. "Agreed," he said. "We'll need to find a better solution. He does pose a risk."

Dixon-Smythe relaxed, as if she was surprised by his agreement. "Once we know how he armed himself," she said, "I want a full report on SGC security."

Chapman nodded at that. "Obviously, he has a contact inside. And, it seems likely that his contact would be someone he knew before…" He waved his hand toward O'Neill. "A friend," he said.

"As I said, once I've debriefed him, I'll investigate how that happened."

"No." Chapman glanced over at Dixon-Smythe and she nodded, as if this was something they'd already agreed. "Not you, General.

We need an impartial audit of this issue, so I'll be appointing General Winchester to oversee that review."

"From Groom Lake?"

Chapman nodded. "He's already expressed some interest in working with the clone."

"And does 'Jonathan O'Neill' get any choice in this?" He sat forward, gaze darting between Chapman and Dixon-Smythe. "Or does he just go where we send him?"

Her smile was chilly. "He'll go where he's most useful. And I expect your plan to reflect that, General. He's a resource. We should use him."

O'Neill swallowed his retort and gave a curt nod. He was backed against the wall and these people didn't even know the half of it. Daniel, Teal'c, Carter: they were all implicated now and he had no idea how he could protect them, and even less how he could protect the clone. But one way or another, he'd do it. He just needed a little time.

"You'll have my recommendations in two weeks," he said, and fixed Dixon-Smythe with his steeliest glare.

Her chin lifted and for a moment he thought she'd give him half that time, but then she closed the slim manila folder in front of her on the table and said, "Very well, we'll look forward to reading them, General. Thank you for your time."

His phone was already in his hand as he left the room. "Lieutenant," he said to his PA. "I need to be on the next flight to Peterson."

There were, Jack well knew, plenty of advantages to the youthful body he found himself inhabiting, and a speedy healing time was one of them. Just a couple days after he'd arrived at the SGC, he found himself being handed a set of BDUs and told to get dressed, despite Dr. Lam's tight looks at the SFs who'd come to escort him.

"I'll need to see him tomorrow," she told them.

The men looked about Jack's age—that is, they were about the age that he appeared to be, but to his older eyes they just looked like kids, scrubbed up and green as grass. Cannon fodder.

"Thanks for patching me up, doc," he said as he left.

"You're welcome. Don't go running any marathons."

His answering smile brought a tint of color to her cheeks. Another thing Jack had noticed about being young again—his smiles were rather more potent than they had been and he couldn't help enjoying that too. Hell, he had to take his fun where he could find it these days.

Despite clearly being under arrest, the moment he stepped out of the infirmary and into the familiar corridor beyond felt like liberation. It felt like all his Christmases come at once.

Nothing much had changed: the same low ceilings, the same gray walls and lines of red paint running along the floor, the same hum of the ventilation system and clump of booted footsteps echoing through the corridors.

He could imagine Carter and Daniel and Teal'c were in their respective labs or quarters, he could imagine that George Hammond was in his office, Dr. Fraiser in the infirmary, but he knew that none of it was true. He'd found out last year that Hammond and Fraiser were dead, that SG-1 as he knew it no longer existed.

He'd asked Dr. Lam if he could see Daniel, or Carter, or Teal'c, but none of them were 'available'. Whatever the hell that meant. Scratch that, he knew *exactly* what it meant. It meant what it had always meant, from the moment he'd first woken up in this new body. It meant that he wasn't Jack O'Neill anymore and that these people he'd fought with and cared about were no longer his friends. He might be back at the SGC—hell, they might have pulled him out of Raqqa themselves—but this was no homecoming.

Like it or not, he was still behind enemy lines and he had no one to trust but himself.

As the car from Peterson swept in through the gates to Cheyenne Mountain, O'Neill felt the anxiety he'd been nurturing the whole way tighten into a definite headache.

It was a pretty apt metaphor for this whole screwed-up situation.

The clone had screwed up big-time, drawing this kind of attention to himself. O'Neill might have been able to shield him if he'd just given name, rank, and serial number, but the zat…? The zat elevated this mess into a whole new league of trouble.

The airman on duty waved them through and moments later O'Neill was in the elevator heading down. The old familiar route still felt like coming home, despite the ten years he'd spent in DC. He figured this place would always feel like home; it was where he'd reshaped his identity and re-found his purpose, where he'd learned to live again, after Charlie's death.

He shifted, suddenly uneasy at the thought of how his clone had been banished from the SGC and how hard that must have been for the kid. "Sonofabitch," he murmured under his breath. Nothing about this situation didn't suck.

Landry met him at the elevator, offered a handshake and a furrowed brow.

"How is he?" O'Neill asked as they walked.

"Healing," Hank said. "He took a beating but he's a young man—" He slid a look at Jack. "These kids heal fast."

"Can't help thinking," O'Neill said, wry, "that he got the better deal outa this whole cloning situation."

Not that he really believed it, and Landry obviously didn't because he just raised one of his impressive eyebrows and said, "He's not so much like you as I'd have thought, Jack."

"Oh?"

He shook his head. "He's… How do I put it? He's sharper, somehow."

"*Smarter?*"

"No!" He huffed out a laugh. "No, I mean his edges are sharper. He looks … Jack, there's something dangerous about him. I don't know. I'm not sure I'd put him in the field."

"That's not even an option."

"Agreed. But I mean … There's a lot of anger there, beneath the surface. Life experience to the contrary, he looks like an angry young man."

O'Neill absorbed that in silence. The guy was, of course, him from his toenails right up to his uncooperative hair. He'd never exactly been an angry young man, but he *had* known what it was to be angry and desperate—desperate enough to take a nuke through the Stargate and not plan on coming home. Yeah, he knew exactly what this guy could be capable of doing. "You're saying," he ventured, as they headed up the stairs to Hank's office, "that we can't just let him walk around out there in the big wide world."

Landry took a breath and let it out as a sigh. "I think he's proven that already, hasn't he?"

"He didn't hurt anyone," O'Neill pointed out, "at least no one—" He stopped talking, distracted for a moment by the sight of the Stargate as they crossed the briefing room toward the general's office. Even now, it had the power to render him speechless.

Hank glanced over and smiled. "It's still got it, huh?"

"Always will," he replied with a smile of his own. But it didn't last long. It seemed like everything now was shadowed by the experience of mini-me, and O'Neill couldn't help but imagine what it would be like to be cut off from all of this. Knowing it was here, knowing the gate was still open, that a galaxy teaming with life and adventure and threat was still out there, and being cut off like a junkie going cold turkey. He thought it would be enough to drive him nuts. Perhaps, literally.

Landry led him into the office and waved him toward the visitor's chair. "We're holding him in VIP quarters," he said, taking his own seat. "Dr. Lam released him from the infirmary yesterday."

"I can imagine he's taking that well."

Landry shrugged. "He's watching a lot of TV and eating cake."

"Sounds about right." He sighed then, ran a finger under his collar. He wished he didn't have to wear his blues; it didn't feel right down here, somehow. "You know," he said, "there's a chance that he didn't intend to come back from his little one-man mission into Syria."

"I considered that." Landry didn't quite meet O'Neill's eye. "I've asked Dr. Mayer to run a psych eval."

"Which will tell us exactly squat. No offense."

Landry spread his hands. "You got a better idea, Jack?"

"I have *no* ideas." He sighed. "But I guess I have to go talk to the guy."

"Well, if anyone can understand him, it's you."

He almost laughed at that. "Don't count on it, Hank. I do a pretty good line in self-deception."

An abrupt rap on the door of the VIP quarters that were serving as his jail disturbed Jack's thoughts, but he didn't get up from where he lay on the bed. Not even when the door opened and one of the nameless SFs stepped inside, coming to parade rest and letting someone else enter.

Top brass, Jack thought, and watched as a three-star general walked into the room.

And then he froze.

"Well," the general said, "this is weird."

Slowly, Jack sat up.

The general nodded to the SF, who promptly left the room and closed the door behind him. In the tight silence that followed, General O'Neill's gaze fixed on Jack. "You've grown," he said.

"And you're gray." Jack got to his feet.

The general—the other Jack O'Neill—dismissed the jibe with a lift of his eyebrows. "So," he said, "let's get down to business. What the *hell* were you thinking?"

"Excuse me?"

"Don't try that crap on me." O'Neill took a step closer, his anger barely contained. "You know exactly what I'm talking about. What the hell were you thinking, going in there alone? And taking a *zat* with you!"

"There were two hostages in that building, *General*," he said. "I went in to get them out."

"*On your own?*"

He folded his arms. "I don't have a team anymore."

"They found your zat," O'Neill retorted. "They put it on YouTube!" Anger hummed beneath the surface. "I repeat: what were you *thinking*?"

Jack sucked in a breath through his nose, schooled himself not to be riled by this guy who'd taken everything from him. "What would you have done? Become a cop? A firefighter, maybe? Volunteered for the Red Cross? Don't think I haven't thought about all of that, *Jack*. But you know what? Screw it. We both know what we are: we're soldiers. We're warriors. And, as it turns out, we can't be anything else."

"Bullshit."

"Is it?" He let his gaze wander over the guy's dress blues, the stars on his shoulder. "Maybe—at your age—it's okay to fly a desk. But I'm not old, General, and I'm not ready. If I can't fight off-world, then I'll fight at home. If I can't join the US military, then I'll damn well do it my own way." He levelled a finger, but held off on jabbing the general in the chest. "You would do the same."

"No," O'Neill said. "I wouldn't."

Jack studied him—that older face, the silver hair, the uniform. "Too much to lose?" He couldn't keep the bitter smile from his lips. "Well, maybe that's where we're different, General."

O'Neill flinched. Jack could see guilt flicker behind his eyes. "I didn't create you," he said. "And I did everything I could to help you."

"Right. Before you took everything—"

"It wasn't yours!" O'Neill snapped. "None of it was yours.

It's *my* life. What the hell else could I have done?"

"You could have let me keep *something*. You could have thrown me a goddamn bone. You could have told me that Hammond had died, that we'd lost Fraiser—you could have *acknowledged* me!"

O'Neill turned away, stalked back toward the door and took a couple of breaths. "This whole situation…"

"Screwed up? Yeah, I know. Welcome to my life."

"You know we can't just leave it like this, right?" O'Neill turned back around and it looked like the fight had gone out of him, like there was a weight on his shoulders that Jack didn't share. "You've screwed up. People are asking questions, and I— I don't have any answers to give them."

Jack spread his hands. "Not my problem."

A slow beat fell. "You're a sonofabitch, you know that?"

"Right back atcha, General."

It wasn't that Daniel was hiding, exactly. It was more that he was keeping a low profile. He'd heard that Jack was on base and didn't relish the conversation to come, so he'd headed down to his lab to do a little research into the problem on Atlantis.

He should have known that wouldn't work.

His coffee wasn't even cool before the phone rang and he was summoned to a meeting in the briefing room. "General O'Neill said not to be late," the harried lieutenant warned.

Daniel huffed out a laugh. "Right. On my way."

He snagged up a notebook, his coffee, and his jacket and made his way out of his lab. He wasn't exactly dawdling, but he wasn't exactly hurrying either. He'd never really gotten used to taking orders from Jack O'Neill, even in the field when it was a matter of life and death, and the older he got the less bothered he was by Jack's narrow-eyed impatience. Besides, he needed a few moments to marshal his thoughts. Someone, he figured, had to stand up for the cloned Jack and he suspected it would probably be him.

He was halfway down the corridor when the base alarms sounded. "Unauthorized off-world activation!"

Standing aside, keeping his out of the fray, he let people rush past him toward the gate room and the control room. Time was when he'd have been the one bolting along the corridor, but much had changed at the SGC since the heydays of SG-1 and there were other—younger—people manning the front line now. Daniel didn't mind that at all, although he suspected that Jack did. Both Jacks, he reflected.

By the time he'd climbed the few narrow stairs into the control room, the iris was shut and Landry was talking to someone on the view screen. Daniel didn't recognize the face, but the uniform told him it was the Atlantis expedition checking in, no doubt chasing their request. His curiosity was piqued, but the control room was crowded and he didn't want to get in the way. Besides, if they needed his input, they'd ask. He felt a twist of guilt, nonetheless; with everything that had hit the fan on their end, it was impossible for Jack to help them. He doubted Landry had even had time to mention their request.

Skirting around the backs of the personnel bent over their computers, Daniel made his way up the spiral stairs and into the briefing room above. He wasn't the first to arrive: Teal'c stood gazing down at the shuttered gate, hands behind his back, still dressed in the clothes he customarily wore when he travelled to Dakara.

"Hey." Daniel dumped his stuff on the briefing room table. "You're back."

Teal'c turned and bowed his head in greeting. "I am."

"How were the talks?"

"Long," Teal'c said and managed to convey more in that single word than most people could say in a sentence.

Daniel smiled and sat down. "At least they're still talking. That's progress."

"It is." Teal'c took a final glance over his shoulder at the Stargate, before he came to join Daniel at the table. "But I understand we have trouble of our own, Daniel Jackson."

He conceded the point with a sigh. "Yeah. Jack's pretty pissed about the zat."

"Giving Jonathan O'Neill the zat'nik'a'tel was … impulsive," Teal'c conceded. "On reflection, I should not have done so."

"Well, it's a moot point."

"Indeed."

"The question is," Daniel said, "what do we do with him now?"

"It is unlikely that you or I will be able to decide his fate," Teal'c said, and Daniel didn't miss the edge of concern in his words. "Even General O'Neill—"

"Even General O'Neill," said a voice from Landry's office, "has no idea what to do with him."

Daniel glanced up. "Jack."

"Daniel." He was leaning on the doorjamb, hands in his pockets. "T. How're you doing?"

"I am well, O'Neill."

"So," Jack said, strolling into the room and helping himself to coffee. "We got ourselves a little problem."

Daniel watched him for a moment—the silver hair, the straight shoulders, the worry creased into his features. And he thought about the other Jack they'd just pulled out of Syria, young and full of angry energy when they'd met last year. It was difficult to reconcile the idea that they were, or at least had been, the same man. "Have you spoken to him?" he said after a pause.

"Yeah," Jack said, turning back around and stirring his coffee. "He's a stubborn bastard."

Daniel almost choked. "Uh, yeah. Well, he is you …"

"You're funny," Jack said with a narrow-eyed look. "But he's way worse than me. He's—"

"Pissed off," Daniel said, his humor fading. "Are you surprised?"

Jack walked to the head of the table, hesitated with a hand

on the back of Landry's customary chair, then took a seat further down the table before he said, "He had a chance to start again, to start over—a new life, Daniel. A second chance at everything."

Daniel was silent, glanced over the table at Teal'c.

"It is not always easy," Teal'c said, in answer to Daniel's look, "to cast off your old life. Even I—" He hesitated, but then said, "When I first came to Earth, the knowledge that I was fighting for my family and for my people gave me comfort. Had I been excluded from that fight, had I believed that my people were no longer mine, that I was no longer part of their world…? It would have been difficult to find meaning in my life."

"I guess we all know something about starting over," Daniel added. "It's fighting for the memory of what you've lost that keeps you going, right? Without that…" He shook his head. "I don't know. I don't know if it's even possible to rebuild."

Jack tapped his fingers on the table, his gaze fixed inward until, in a tense voice, he said, "He can't just have my life."

"No one's saying that."

"Then what?" He looked up and fixed Daniel with a hard look. "What are you saying? Because that guy? He's not me. He's— He's someone else now. And he can't stay here."

"But where else *can* he go?" Daniel countered. "Tell me, Jack. You can't keep him locked up for the rest of his life."

"And we can't arm him and let him loose like *Rambo*!" He leaned forward, voice lowered and angry. "He's a danger, Daniel—to himself, to the people around him. And, most importantly, to the whole Stargate program. We don't know for sure what he told his interrogators." He tapped his head. "The stuff he knows, Daniel… It could break this thing wide open. It could destroy everything if it falls into the wrong hands."

"Yeah, I know." Daniel sighed because there was no getting around that.

"He had one job," Jack continued in that low, angry voice. "Keep his head down. That was it. And what does he do?"

Shaking his head he sat back, lips pressed into a tight line. "Stupid sonofabitch."

Teal'c shifted in his seat. "I feel I am partially to blame for the situation," he confessed. "It was I who encouraged him to involve himself in the problems of this world. And it was I who gave him the zat'nik'a'tel."

Jack didn't answer that, just kept tapping out an angry tattoo with his fingers on the table with that tight, inward look. Knowing him as well as he did, Daniel wondered exactly how much blame for this whole situation Jack was placing on himself. After all, he'd been the one to send the kid out there alone eleven years ago, and really, they should have seen this coming all along. No one puts Jack O'Neill in a corner.

"The IOA want to bury him," Jack said at last. "Want to send him to Area 51, or—I don't know—somewhere he can be 'useful'."

Daniel blew out a low breath. "Useful?"

"Yeah." Jack shook his head again. "If he'd just kept his head down ... But the genie's out the bottle now."

General Landry huffed his way up the steps from the control room, breaking the tense silence that had fallen. "Apologies." He looked harried and glanced out at the Stargate as he passed the window. Its iris was sliding open, the wormhole disengaged.

"Problems?" Jack's gaze followed Landry's.

"Always," the general said with a tense smile. "A situation on Atlantis."

Jack's eyebrows rose, mouth opening as if to speak, but then he snapped it shut. "Let me know if I need to know."

"Of course." Landry exchanged half a glance at Daniel as he took his seat at the head of the table. "Now, any ideas what we're going to do with our visitor?"

There followed a long moment full of silent looks, but Daniel found his own gaze drifting out past Teal'c to the silent Stargate. He heard Jack speak, but didn't catch his words, because his mind had started to run in a new direction. Somewhere useful, Jack had said...

"I've got it," he blurted, cutting across whatever Teal'c had been saying.

They all looked at him. Landry blinked, "Excuse me, Dr. Jackson?"

"Uh," Daniel shook his head to clear it, sitting up a little straighter in his chair. "Sorry. I mean— They need Jack on Atlantis, right?"

"Dr. Jackson." Landry scowled a warning, his brow drawn low over his eyes. "That is *not* the subject of this meeting."

"No. I know, it's just—" He held up a hand to cut off further protest. "Don't you see? We could kill two birds with one stone. Ah, or rather, save two birds with one stone, to extend the metaphor."

"I don't think—"

"Stop." Jack held up a hand. "Just— Back up." He fixed a look on Landry. "Hank, what are we talking about? What's happening on Atlantis?"

Landry threw a final, hard look at Daniel, then said, "Colonel Sheppard has had a run-in with one of those Ancient Repository—"

"You mean a head-sucker?" Jack said, with a wincing glance at Daniel.

He nodded. "And without the Asgard around to download the data from his brain…" He left that hanging, because Jack understood what it meant better than anyone.

Tension creased around his eyes. "And I can help how, exactly?"

"We don't know that you can," Landry said. "But Dr. Beckett, Atlantis's CMO, thinks it might be possible to use your brain as a … as some kind of blueprint to allow the Ancient device to re-upload the data from Colonel Sheppard." He threw a pointed look at Daniel. "Obviously, it would be too big of a risk, which is why I hadn't mentioned it, given the current crisis."

"Ah!" Daniel said, and couldn't help the beat of triumph that pumped in his chest. "But that's just my point. This could actually solve *both* crises."

"Both?" Landry traded a confused look with Jack. "Dr. Jackson, what are you—?"

"No," Jack said almost at the same moment. "Daniel, no."

"Come on," he pressed. "Why not?"

"Why not? Where shall I *start*?"

"Excuse me," Landry objected. "What are we talking about?"

Jack glared at Daniel and he held his look without any trouble. He'd been glared at by Jack O'Neill more times than he could remember.

"I believe," Teal'c said, when neither of them spoke, "that Daniel Jackson is suggesting that the cloned O'Neill travel to Atlantis in an endeavor to help Colonel Sheppard."

"It's a stupid idea," Jack said, jaw set and arms folded. "It's not gonna happen."

"Well you can't go," Daniel said. "And if they don't find a solution, Sheppard will die."

"The clone," Jack said, very deliberately, "is not going off-world."

Daniel held his gaze a beat longer before he turned in appeal to Landry. "Think about it," he said. "If there's some kind of Asgard programming in Jack's brain then the clone will have it too—plus, and probably more importantly—it gets him out from under the IOA. He can do his job out there, he can make a difference." He fixed another look on Jack. "He can be *useful*."

"The IOA would never go for it."

"So tell them when it's done. Present them with a *fait accompli*."

Jack's expression set harder. "Daniel—"

"Just think about it, Jack. He'd be a whole galaxy away. He wouldn't be taking your life, but he'd still be part of the Stargate program. He'd still be fighting, using his skills, making a difference. It's— look, you said it yourself, the stuff he knows could blow the whole Stargate program apart. And we know he won't—he *can't*—just sit at home and pretend that part of his life never happened. He can't do it. You couldn't do it and it's not fair to expect him to."

"Daniel—"

"You know it, Jack. You know it's true."

Jack blew out a breath and was silent, thinking. Into the silence, Landry said, "It may not be that simple, Dr. Jackson."

"Why not?"

"Because—"

"Because he's nuts," Jack said, grinding the words out between his teeth.

"Nuts?"

"Angry," he conceded. "And with nothing left to lose." He fixed Daniel with a dark look, a look that took him back a couple decades to Abydos and to the Jack O'Neill he'd first met. A man with nothing left to lose and a nuke in his back pocket. "He's capable of anything, Daniel. He shouldn't be in the field."

Daniel nodded, not so much because he agreed about the clone but because he understood where Jack was coming from. "But that's the thing," he countered. "We'd be giving him something worth losing—a cause, a home, a place where he can be himself again. A place where he can, maybe, really start his life again."

Another tense silence welled up between them. Jack's expression was taut, but Daniel could tell he was considering the possibility.

"Atlantis," Landry said after a beat, "isn't a place for us to dump our problems, Dr. Jackson. You know that better than anyone. It's a frontline operation. They need the best people out there."

"Jack O'Neill is the best," Teal'c said, chin lifting in defiance as if waiting for O'Neill to argue. "The clone has all his skills, his knowledge, and a younger and stronger body with which to use them."

"Hey," Jack objected, but only half-heartedly.

"It would be foolish to waste his talents," Teal'c continued, "if there is a chance that he can use them to benefit your people."

"Teal'c's right," Daniel said. "And isn't that what the IOA wants? For him to be useful? At least give him a chance, Jack. Send him to help Sheppard, see how he does—see how he fits in with the Atlantis expedition. It can't hurt, right?"

"It can't hurt? Daniel, he could get someone killed."

"You really think that?"

"I— I don't know. That's my problem."

A beat fell, full of tension and indecision. "He's already undergoing to a full psych assessment," Landry said, with a glance at O'Neill. "As much as you don't like them, Jack, it will tell us something."

Jack rubbed a hand across his face, shook his head. "I don't like any of this."

Daniel felt like he was holding his breath as he glanced over at Teal'c who simply lifted an eyebrow. *Wait*, he seemed to say. *Wait...*

"But," Jack went on with a sigh, "as far as plans go, so far it's the only one we have that doesn't involve burying him in a deep dark hole or handing him over to Area 51."

"So is that a yes?"

"Yeah," Jack said. "Go ahead and ask him. See what he thinks."

"Ask him?" And there were times, even after all these years, when Jack managed to surprise him. "Ask mini-you?"

"Why not? It's his life. He should be able to choose which crappy fate he'd prefer."

"Atlantis isn't a crappy fate."

"Isn't it? We're asking him to go to another galaxy and risk his life for a guy he's never met. Either that, or spend the rest of his life like a chimp in a lab." Jack scowled, but Daniel could tell the expression was turned inward, that he was blaming himself for not finding a better option. "Some choice."

"I know what I'd choose," Daniel said. "Risk or not."

"Yeah, but that's the point, isn't it? It's not really a choice at all. Not when there's a man's life at stake. Not when the other option is worse."

The truth of that made something squirm in the pit of Daniel's stomach. "I think we just have to consider this the least worst option," he said. "There are no good outcomes here."

Jack's lips tightened, his slight nod acknowledging the point.

"Tell you what," Daniel said, "why don't I go with him to Atlantis? Keep an eye on things."

"What, you're a brain-science specialist now?" Jack said, with a tilt of his mouth. Almost a smile.

"No," he said. "But I'm something of a Jack O'Neill specialist…"

Teal'c smiled at that and so did Landry. Jack just narrowed his eyes, but Daniel saw no bite there. Jack knew exactly what he meant. "Fine," he said. "Go with him, be his guardian angel."

Daniel lifted his eyebrows. "Okay. Maybe tell the IOA I'm there to provide oversight or something?"

Pushing his chair back and standing up, Jack said, "Just make sure he doesn't screw anything else up."

"It'll be okay. *He'll* be okay."

Jack held his gaze for a beat with a look that was something halfway between 'I hope you're right' and 'I trust you', then he turned to Landry. "I need to get back to DC. Keep me apprised."

"Jack?" Daniel got to his feet as Jack headed for the stairs. "For what it's worth, I think you made the right call."

He turned at the top of the stairs, one hand on the railing. "Tell me that after you get back, Daniel. Then I might believe it."

# CHAPTER THREE

"ANOTHER galaxy, you say?"

"It's called Pegasus," Daniel explained from where he leaned against the wall in Jack's quarters/cell. "It's where the Ancients went when they left Earth. We have a base in one of their abandoned cities…" His eyebrows twitched, brow wrinkling. "It's, uh, it's actually called Atlantis."

Jack couldn't keep the sardonic twist from his lips. "As in 'The Lost City of…'?"

"Yep. That's the one."

"Correct me if I'm wrong, but I thought Atlantis sank."

"Turns out it did." Daniel pushed himself off the wall and dropped into one of the plastic chairs on the other side of the table from where Jack sat with his feet propped up. "We—that is, the Atlantis Expedition—raised the city. That was nine years ago now."

Jack huffed out a laugh. "You do realize that sounds like bullshit?"

"More so than an alien portal that lets you travel between planets?"

He shrugged, conceding the point, and fixed his old friend with a steady look. "So what's it got to do with me?"

"There may be an opening there, for you."

For a moment he just stared, not quite taking it in. "Come again?"

"An opening," Daniel said, slowly, like he was talking to a child. "One of the Atlantis team is in trouble. And you…" He shrugged. "Well, you have something they need, so I thought— That is, *we* thought this would be an opportunity for you to … to find a place for yourself."

"In another galaxy." He lifted an eyebrow. "Another *galaxy*, Daniel."

Daniel spread his hands, pressing them flat on the table. "Pegasus is an incredible place, Jack. And Atlantis …? You've never seen anything like it. It's beautiful, powerful—oh, and it's a ship as well as a city. Did I mention that? I mean the thing *flies*. It's how the Ancients left Earth, actually, and it's—" He smiled, obviously reigning in the enthusiasm. "Look, trust me, this is an incredible opportunity."

"Sure," Jack said, playing it cool even if his heartbeat had kicked up a notch at this unexpected offer. "An incredible opportunity for General O'Neill to get rid of me."

Daniel tipped his head, brow furrowing in irritation. "Actually, he was opposed to the idea. If it makes you feel any better, I had to talk him into it."

"And why would you do that?"

Daniel let out a slow breath, steepling his fingers and looking at Jack over their tips. "Because, no matter what you might think, I'm still your friend. And because I know that this is your best—probably your only—shot at getting back into the game."

Swinging his feet down from the table, Jack stood up and paced toward the locked door. "And what is it they need from me? I'm guessing it's not my winning sense of humor."

"No. It's something in your brain. Something we think the Asgard may have left there when they were removing the Ancient database you downloaded the first time."

Jack's mind snagged on that for a moment. "The *first* time?"

"Ah, yeah, he did it again. Long story, but the point is that they need you on Atlantis."

"Why me?" he said. "Why me and not him?"

There was a long pause. He could hear Daniel shifting in his chair, a low clearing of his throat before he spoke. "Because," he said at last, "it's too dangerous. We can't risk him."

A bitter smile crept onto Jack's face. "Ah. I get it. I'm expendable."

"That's not how—"

"And if I say no?" He kept his back turned as he asked the question, not wanting to see Daniel's reaction.

"Then… Then, actually, I don't know," he said. "Jack— General O'Neill—won't just let you walk out of here. The IOA won't permit it, not after what you did in Syria. Too many people are asking questions now. Besides, you present a risk."

Jack swung around to face him. "The hell I do."

"The things you know, Jack…"

"I'm not gonna tell anyone about the Stargate program, for cryin' out loud."

Daniel gave him an appraising look. "I think we both know that you might, under enough pressure."

Jack felt himself pale, felt the blood drain from his face. Daniel, after all, was the only one who knew how close he'd gotten to giving up in those dark days and weeks he'd been held prisoner by Ba'al. The muscles in his jaw jumped with tension. "That's low, Daniel."

"But you know it's true." Daniel's gaze remained cool and unblinking. "And so does General O'Neill."

Jack just stared at him for a long moment, processing that fact. He'd die before he'd betray the SGC, but he knew that sometimes death wasn't an option and that in the end everybody talked. It was just a question of how long you held out.

"This is what you've been asking for," Daniel pressed, turning in his seat to look at him straight. "It's a second chance to contribute."

"If I survive the head-sucking thing again."

"Every time you step through the gate, there's a risk," Daniel said. "And the threat to Earth doesn't just stop at the edge of the Milky Way. We've already faced an incursion from another galaxy, and the situation in Pegasus is precarious. You could make a difference there."

And, he supposed, that was the point. That chance of making a difference was what made his blood race and his heart pound at the prospect of getting into the field again—even if it was a field in a distant galaxy. "So, uh, the bad guys in Pegasus?" he said. "What are we talking about? Goa'ulds?"

Daniel gave a bleak smile. "They're called Wraith," he said, and lifted his hand in a claw-like gesture. "They can, ah, suck out your life force in a matter of seconds."

Jack cocked a wry eyebrow. "Space vampires?"

"You're gonna love 'em."

Two hours after Daniel had left his quarters, Jack found himself back in the locker room he remembered so well, gearing up for a mission. He was doing a pretty good job of showing the world his usual flip ambivalence, but sitting alone in such a familiar place he couldn't deny the poignancy of the moment. After ten long years in the wilderness, he was home. Kinda.

The lockers were the same, although the names on them had changed over the years. But he instinctively found his way over to the one that had once been his and cast his eyes over what had been Daniel's, Teal'c's, and Carter's. He knew nothing would ever compare with those glory days of SG-1, but as he looked down at the new uniform they'd provided for him, a crisp new SGC patch on his arm, he had to allow himself a smile of triumph.

He was back.

And, considering where he'd been just a couple of weeks ago, this was as close to miraculous as things got. He dressed quickly and glanced at himself in the bathroom mirror before he left. He'd gotten used to this young face and seeing himself back in uniform gave his stomach a sharp little twist of … what was that? Gratitude? He was young, he was strong, and he was about to step through the Stargate again. He was about to travel to another galaxy. "Holy crap," he told his reflection. "You're one lucky bastard."

Daniel was waiting in the corridor outside the locker room, and Jack was surprised to see him dressed for the field too. "I'm coming with you," Daniel explained when he saw Jack's surprise.

"Babysitter?"

He shrugged. "I'll take any opportunity to visit Atlantis. It never gets old." Then he paused, glanced down the corridor and back to Jack. "So," he said, more seriously. "Ready for this?"

"For the last ten years," Jack said, but even so his pulse was racing as they turned toward the gate room. Every step was familiar, the corridors crowded with ghosts and memories. Daniel was talking, but Jack was only half listening and tuned him out completely as they turned the corner into the final corridor and his gaze fixed on the blast doors at the end. How often had he walked or run toward those doors, fought to hold them shut? His mouth felt dry, his heart pounding behind his ribs as the doors swung open ahead of him and that familiar static ozone scent of the gate room filled his head.

And there it was. There it was again: the Stargate.

Jack stopped dead, just inside the doors, only peripherally aware of the team waiting at the foot of the ramp, of Daniel slowing and turning back around toward him as Jack stared up at the silent Stargate. It was bigger than he'd remembered, dominating the room, and the ache of familiarity made him catch his breath.

"Jack?" Daniel's voice was quiet, respectful.

"Uh, yeah," he said, not taking his eyes from the gate. "I just— I never thought I'd see it again."

Daniel came back to stand with him and Jack felt his shoulder brush against his own, brothers-in-arms as they'd once been. "A long ten years," Daniel said.

"A lifetime." He glanced sideways at his friend—different from the man he'd known, older, less troubled—and knew there was no going back. Everything but the Stargate had changed, including himself. "So," he said, clearing his throat, "thirty-four gates?"

Daniel gave a smile. "Thirty-four."

"Cool."

With a nod of his head, Daniel drew him over toward the

team waiting for them. "This is Colonel Novak," Daniel said, introducing a serious looking dark-haired man a couple inches shorter than Jack. "Leader of SG-19—covert ops. They're going to get us in."

Jack pegged Novak in his late thirties, which was older than Jack looked but younger than he felt. He'd never get used to that weird contradiction. "Colonel," he said with a nod. He didn't salute; he wasn't military anymore.

Novak gave a nod in return, his sharp gaze running over Jack's uniform. "I heard a lot about you, O'Neill." He fixed Jack with an intent look. "You gonna be able to follow my orders?"

Jack glanced over at Daniel, who was watching him with an equally intent expression. And, although he didn't look up at the window to the control room, he'd have bet the farm on the fact that O'Neill and Landry were watching him too. So, really, there was only one answer to give if he wanted to step through that gate. "Yes sir," he said and waved a hand at the empty spaces on his uniform. "I don't have a rank anymore ..."

Novak's gaze darted to the control room and back. "Well," he said, "let's see if you earn one."

"Is that how it works, these days?"

"In your case," Novak said, with a slight smile, "I think they're throwing the rule book out the window."

Jack exchanged a look with Daniel, who just shrugged. "Don't ask me," he said. "I'm still not military."

From behind them, Landry's voice came over the microphone. "Colonel Novak, is your team ready?"

Novak shot a final look at Jack, and then turned to the window. "Yes sir."

Jack followed his gaze and saw that he'd been half right. Landry was watching, but there was no sign of O'Neill. Teal'c stood behind the general too, and raised a hand in both greeting and farewell when he saw Jack looking. He mirrored the gesture.

"Then you have a go, SG-19," Landry said into the mic. "And

good luck—all of you."

A moment later, the gate began to spin and Jack turned to watch with a churn of anticipation. It was exactly how he remembered it, all barely contained power and unknown potential. When it reached chevron five, he glanced over at Daniel.

"Get ready," Daniel said, adjusting his glasses. "It's quite a ride."

"And this really works?" Jack said, turning back to watch the eighth chevron lock. "Thirty-four different Stargates."

"And the Midway station too," Daniel said. "And of course it works. Sam built it."

"Naturally." He cast a quick, self-conscious glance at Daniel. "Uh, so how is Carter anyway?"

"Good," Daniel said, keeping his gaze fixed on the Stargate. "She's on her final mission in command of the *Hammond*, actually. She's about to be promoted. Again."

He didn't have much to say to that. Carter's stellar rise through the ranks was a given. But there was a fuzzy memory in the back of his mind from the day he was rescued from Syria that he couldn't shake: blonde hair, camouflage paint, the authority of command. He was about to ask Daniel if she'd been there, if Carter had come to pull him out, but at that moment the seventh chevron locked and the wormhole flooded out into the room.

It was just as beautiful as he remembered, just as awesome in a very literal sense. "Cool," he breathed, because what else was there to say? There were no words to adequately express how much this moment meant to him.

"SG-19," Novak said, heading up the ramp, "O'Neill, Dr. Jackson—move out."

The rest of the team fell in behind the colonel, but Jack hung back for a moment. He couldn't help glancing over his shoulder, taking a final look around the gate room, up at the control room—at Teal'c and Landry, and the other less familiar faces.

*I might never come back.* The thought drove into him like

an arrow, like the thing that had once pierced his shoulder and pinned him to the wall of this very room so many years ago. *I might never see this place again.*

"Jack?" Daniel touched his arm. "Come on, time to go."

"Yeah," he said with a nod, turning his back on the control room—on Earth. Time for a new adventure, time for a new life. Even so, he couldn't help the pang in the pit of his stomach as he stepped up onto the ramp, his boots sounding that familiar metallic clang as he walked toward the open wormhole. He stopped, just momentarily, on the cusp, remembering Carter doing the same thing that first time she'd stepped through the gate. So long ago now, literally in another life…

And then he took a breath, braced his shoulders, and took the final step. With Daniel at his shoulder, he embraced the old, familiar sensation of plummeting in pieces through spacetime. If he could have, he'd have whooped with the sheer exhilaration of the ride.

A moment later, he found himself stepping back into reality—an echoing space of cool blue and white light, sinuous lines and a distinctly alien feel. It was a large room, with a wide staircase leading up to a kind of mezzanine level, and a low buzz of energy he could feel through the souls of his boots, brushing static across his skin. Ahead of him, just reaching the bottom of the steps, were two figures: a large man with a mass of dark hair, and a woman whose slight build defied her obvious strength. Neither of them wore anything that resembled a uniform.

Novak took a step forward. "Teyla, Ronon," he said. "Good to see you."

"Colonel," the woman said with a polite nod. "Thank you for coming. We were very pleased to get General Landry's message…" Her gaze flitted through the rest of the team, over Daniel, and landed on Jack with reserved curiosity.

Taking the hint, Daniel stepped forward. "Jack," he said, "this is Teyla Emmagan and Ronon Dex. They're friends and team-mates of Colonel Sheppard."

"Hey," Jack said, with a nod to each.

Ronon simply folded his arms, regarding Jack with overt suspicion, but Teyla took a step closer and offered a smile. "We are very grateful to you for coming."

"Are you sure it'll work for him?" Ronon said, directing his words to Novak.

Novak gave a shrug. "I'm no doctor," he said. "But the egg-heads at the SGC think so. He's an exactly copy, remember."

"*He's* standing right here," Jack groused, which earned him a look from Novak that was half irritation and half chagrin. Jack ignored it and focused on Ronon instead. "Like it or not," he said, "I'm what you've got."

He felt Daniel's hand on his shoulder then, a calming gesture. "We know from the tests run when Jack, ah, first showed up, that the cloning process used DNA that was taken from Jack sometime after his first run-in with the Ancient Repository," he said. "So his DNA will reflect any cellular alterations that the device made to the structure of his brain."

"They're right," came another voice and Jack looked up to see a man trotting down the steps. Middle-aged, dark haired he smiled as he approached. "I've taken a look at the files Dr. Lam sent through," he said, "and the changes have definitely manifested in the cloned brain." He smiled at Jack, then, and said, "Sorry to talk about you in the third person, son." He held out his hand, "I'm Dr. Beckett, Atlantis's CMO."

Jack looked at it, and then shook it. "Jack."

"Aye," he said, "so you are." He held onto his hand a beat longer than comfortable, his gaze locked as if he was looking for something in Jack's face. Then he blinked, looked away and dropped his hand to rub his own together. "Well, we're all here. Shall we get going?"

The woman, Teyla, glanced up at the control room and gave a nod that looked like an order. A moment later, the Stargate began to dial. It wasn't like the gate on Earth, or any other gate he'd ever seen, come to that. It was slicker, less noisy, and a little less impressive. He figured it was some kind of upgrade: Stargate 2.0.

Novak took point, his team fanning out. Ronon was a step behind the colonel and Jack and Daniel were shepherded into the center of the group. "Um," Jack said, glancing around, "can't help but notice I'm unarmed."

"You're a civilian," Novak said, without looking back.

"So's Daniel."

"We're here to keep you safe." Novak adjusted his weapon as the final chevron locked. "Just stay close, kid."

Jaw clenched, he ground out, "Don't call me 'kid'."

"Sorry," Daniel said, from where he stood next to him. "General O'Neill's orders."

"Figures." It was pretty clear it would be helpful to a lot of people if he didn't make it back from this mission. Sending him, unarmed, behind enemy lines would certainly help that agenda. Too bad for them that Jack didn't plan on dying here, or anywhere else for that matter.

The wormhole opened with its usual kawoosh, dazzling and miraculous, and then settled inside the gate. "The Ancient Repository is some distance from the Stargate," Teyla said, "but the planet has been unoccupied since the last cull. With luck, we will avoid notice by the Wraith. There is nothing left to attract them to this world."

"Aside from the Ancient Repository?" Daniel said as Novak gave the signal to move out.

Teyla walked next to them, her P90 held with the kind of ease that suggested familiarity. "It is unlikely," she said, after a thoughtful pause, "that the Repository would attract them. Although I have certainly come across many Wraith for whom the pursuit of knowledge is almost as great a need as their drive to feed."

"On humans?" Jack clarified, still musing over the term 'cull'.

Teyla gave a slight nod.

"So we're talking space-vampire-geeks, now?"

Her expression remained impassive, save the slight lift of an eyebrow in Daniel's direction.

"You'll get used to him," Daniel said, one hand on Jack's shoulder as they approached the event horizon. "Eventually."

And with a gentle shove, he was streaming through the wormhole again and out onto a chill, cloudy world of distant mountains and a sparse scattering of trees. Instinct made him reach for his absent weapon and he dropped into a defensive crouch anyway, making a swift survey of their surroundings. They were in a rough clearing that might once have been ceremonial. He could see a number of stones, some fallen, others overgrown, placed in a circle around the gate and a few stones too regular to be natural littered the ground. Perhaps, once, it had been a pavement.

Novak's team had already spread out and he sensed Daniel, and the three people from Atlantis, leave the gate behind him. A moment later it shut down and the only sound was the subdued chirrup of birdsong and the sigh of wind through trees.

"How long did you say this place had been abandoned?" Daniel said.

"A generation, at least," Teyla said.

"That's unusual, isn't it? For the Wraith to cull a planet to extinction?"

"Yes," Teyla conceded as she stepped down from the platform that held the Stargate. "They usually leave enough survivors to repopulate each world before the next cull. But it's also possible that the people simply choose to leave in the aftermath."

"To go somewhere safer?"

"Of course."

Daniel gave a speculative hum low in his throat and Jack picked up the thought. "Makes you wonder," he said, "why they thought this place was more dangerous than anywhere else. I mean, if these 'Wraith' weren't due to come back, wouldn't it be safer here than anywhere else?"

Teyla stopped her perusal of the clearing, fixed him with a steady look. "People do not always act rationally. Surely, you know that?"

He conceded the point with a shrug, but sent a quick glance over to Daniel. His thoughtful frown set something itching between Jack's shoulder blades; it was one of those frowns that meant Daniel thought there was something else going on here. He'd learned over the seven years he'd been in the field with the guy, that Daniel's instincts were usually right.

He repressed a sigh, and the instinct to start giving orders, and just said, "We should keep our eyes open, anyway. For anything hinky."

"This is Pegasus," Ronon rumbled from where he still stood next to the gate. "If you don't keep your eyes open, you'll die."

Jack had to suppress a smile. The guy sounded so much like Teal'c it was painful. "I'll keep that in mind, big guy," he said, and headed off to join Novak. There was no point in getting sentimental, and Ronon made a good point. If he wanted to get out of this alive, and, more importantly, free, he had to stay sharp.

He had to stay sharper than anyone else on this rock—and that included his so-called friends.

# CHAPTER FOUR

"GENERAL O'Neill?" Lieutenant Liu appeared at the door, his normally calm face unsettled.

"What's up?" O'Neill said, glancing past his assistant and into the office beyond. Then he saw what was up. "Oh."

"Mr. Coolidge just showed up, sir," Liu said. "He didn't call, or I'd have—"

O'Neill waved his apology away and rose to his feet. "Don't worry about it," he said, and through the glass wall of his office made eye-contact with James Coolidge, US representative to the IOA. "Show him in."

"Yes sir. Shall I cancel your two o'clock?"

"Not yet," O'Neill said, allowing himself a wry smile. "With luck, he won't be here that long."

He stayed on his feet while Liu showed Coolidge inside, settling his face into bland professionalism. His own dealings with Coolidge had been slight, but he knew from Carter that the guy was—or at least had been—a sexist jerk with a prejudice against their off-world allies. What he was doing here today, unannounced, O'Neill didn't know but he imagined it had something to do with the whole clone train-wreck.

"General," Coolidge said as he stepped inside, glancing over his shoulder as Liu closed the door. "Thank you for making time to see me."

"Sure," O'Neill said, and gestured to the visitor's chair. "You know me, always happy to see the IOA." His smile, he hoped, wasn't entirely facetious.

Coolidge cleared his throat, his bald head gleaming a little in the overhead light as he sat down. "I'm not here officially," he said, drawing the chair closer to O'Neill's desk. "And I'd like to keep our discussion off the record."

O'Neill considered that a moment, then nodded and sat

down, elbows on the table. "Okay," he said. "Shoot."

"It's…" He glanced to the side, brow knitted, as if wondering where to start. "You may have heard," he said, "that I'm somewhat hard-nosed when it comes to the Atlantis Expedition."

"Somewhat," O'Neill agreed, "in the sense that you wanted to kick out all the off-world personnel."

Coolidge frowned, pressed two fingers to the bridge of his nose. "Yes. Well, that was then. Before Teal'c and Ronon Dex helped to save my life, and to save the SGC from a Wraith incursion."

O'Neill raised his eyebrows. "Okay. And so…?"

"I'm here to warn you," Coolidge said, lowering his voice. "The committee isn't happy with your decision to send the clone to Atlantis."

"Color me surprised."

"They're passing a resolution to make him an asset under their control."

"An asset? He's a *person*."

Coolidge spread his hands. "Not to them. To them he's a resource and they don't trust you, or, frankly, anyone in the Stargate Program, to use him wisely."

"They need him on Atlantis," O'Neill pointed out, keeping his voice even despite the way his heartrate was accelerating. "That's why we sent him there. Colonel Sheppard—"

"You don't have to convince me," Coolidge said. "That's why I'm here, to give you the heads up. The moment he steps back through the gate, he's their property."

"He's nobody's property. With all due respect, screw that."

"I thought you might think so."

O'Neill scratched a hand through his hair. "And you can't talk them out of this?"

"Maybe. But probably not. Aurelia Dixon-Smythe doesn't like you, and she's got a lot of power on the committee right now."

"I noticed, on both counts."

"So," Coolidge said, sitting back in his chair. "Over to you, Jack."

"And what am I supposed to do about it?" He had a few ideas but he'd played this game far too long to admit anything to this man, no matter how much they seemed to be on the same page. "I can't countermand the IOA."

For a moment they just looked at each other, everything unspoken. Then Coolidge nodded and rose to his feet. "It's been good talking to you, General."

"You too," O'Neill agreed, also standing. "Thanks for stopping by."

Coolidge headed toward the door, but stopped before he opened it. "I hope the mission to retrieve Colonel Sheppard is a success," he said. "He's a good officer."

"He is."

"And I hope nothing … bad … happens to the clone. It would be a great loss to the Stargate Program if he didn't make it back."

O'Neill kept his face carefully neutral and only said, "Yes. A great loss."

He sat down slowly when Coolidge had gone, sank back into his chair and closed his eyes. There was a knot of tension at the back of his neck and a sickly twist in the pit of his stomach. There was no way he was letting this clone—this *man*, a version of himself—be turned into anyone's property. It wasn't going to happen. He just had to figure out a way to make sure of that without bringing the wrath of the IOA down on the heads of everyone who was trying to help the kid.

"Sir?" Liu poked his head around the door. "Do you need anything?"

*My team*, he thought. *SG-1. Someone I can trust.* But all he said was, "A coffee wouldn't hurt."

By nightfall, they were nearly halfway to the Ancient Repository and Novak kept them walking another couple hours before he called a halt.

"We should just keep going," Ronon objected when they

stopped. "Sheppard doesn't have much time."

Jack, although he would never admit it out loud, was grateful for the rest. He'd barely recovered from the abuse he'd suffered in Raqqa and, bruised ribs aside, the short rations had depleted a lot of his energy. Not to mention given him the appetite of a hungry horse. Even the thought of MREs was appealing.

"In our experience," Daniel said, dropping his pack with a grunt of relief, "he'll have a couple more days before things are critical."

Ronon cast him a dour look from behind the fall of his dreadlocked hair. "In my experience," he said, "if something needs doing, better to just do it."

"Aye, well," Dr. Beckett chipped in, "don't forget you've got me along for the ride and I'm afraid I need wee sit down."

That, it seemed, was enough to quell Ronon's objections. Jack supposed he trusted his own people more than those from the SGC, and he understood that. Your people were your people. But it plucked at something in his chest, a hollow space where his people should be. He glanced over at Daniel who was rummaging in his pack, pulling out a flashlight. Once upon a time Daniel had been his people, but now… Not that he didn't trust the guy, it was just that he knew he had other priorities—the *real* Jack O'Neill, for a start.

Teyla assured them it was safe to make a fire, and as it cracked merrily it reminded Jack of a hundred other nights off-world with his team. Teal'c would be sitting opposite, lost in kelnoreem. Daniel would probably have his nose buried in one of the books he'd insisted on lugging around with him. (This time, Jack noticed, his nose was buried in an e-reader.) And Carter would be poking at the fire with a stick, rambling on about her theories about their current mission/desperate situation. He'd not valued those nights, that quiet comradeship, enough. He'd have held onto it a helluva lot tighter if he'd known how easily it could all be taken away.

"Hey," Daniel said, nudging Jack's foot with his boot. "You okay?"

"Peachy."

Daniel fixed him with a look that said he didn't buy it, then nodded at the MRE Jack was holding. "What do you think? They gotten any better in the last ten years?"

"I'm liking the beef brisket," Jack said, grateful that Daniel hadn't pressed for more. "That's new."

"Progress, huh?"

Another voice said, "I like the Lemon Pepper Tuna," and Jack glanced over at the doc from Atlantis. "Although," he added, "you can't beat neeps 'n' tatties on a cold night."

Jack blinked at him. "Neeps— What?"

"Come by some time," he said, his smile a gleam of white in the firelight. "I'll show you. *Tuttleroot* makes a decent stand-in for turnips." His smile dimmed a little. "Close as I'm likely to get, anyhow."

Next to him, Jack sensed Daniel shift a little. "We, ah, could send some through the gate. From Earth."

Beckett laughed. "Aye, well, if there's room in the next supply run for turnips, why not?"

It was pretty clear that Jack was missing at least half of the conversation, but he was tired and not in the mood to investigate the significance of turnips. Instead, he finished his meal in a couple of bites and dug out his bed roll. "I'm gonna turn in," he said, and then glanced over at Novak. "Unless you want me to take a turn on watch?"

Novak just said, "We've got it covered."

Which was code for, *Like hell, buddy.* Jack just shrugged. He'd not expected anything different. "Guess I get a whole night's sleep then."

The ground was hard, but not as hard as it had felt when his body had been older. He'd learned to look for positives where he could, and this was another advantage of the young man's body he now owned. Counting the pros helped him forget the incalculable cons of the hand life had dealt him. Pulling his watch cap down over his ears and eyes, he settled down in his bedroll to sleep. That was one thing that hadn't changed—his ability to sleep on demand was legendary.

So was his ability to go from asleep to full alert in less than a second.

Which was why he sat bolt upright some hours later, staring over the fire's embers at Teyla pushing to her feet in alarm. Her sharp intake of breath must have woken him. "What?" he said, voice gravelly.

Her eyes were wide, just a glint in the dim light. "Wraith," she hissed. "There are Wraith here."

Jack was on his feet, scrambling out of his bedroll, heart racing. "Where?" Daniel's P90 lay next to him and Jack had it in his hands before his friend had begun to stir. "Do you see them?"

"It's okay." Teyla held out a pacifying hand. "They're some distance away yet."

"Jack?" Daniel blinked at him, sitting up and reaching for his weapon. "What's going on?"

"Wraith," Teyla said again, tipping her face to the sky. "There are Wraith on the surface."

Confused, Jack said, "And how do you know?"

"I can sense them." She closed her eyes, briefly. "I can feel their presence."

Jack almost snorted. "Really? Like the force?"

Teyla stared at him for a moment, her head tipped sideways. "What force do you mean?"

Before Jack could reply, Novak lifted a hand for silence and toggled his radio to contact the team holding the gate. "Collins, Novak. Sitrep."

The radio crackled, and a moment later Collin's staticy voice replied, "*Novak, Collins. All good, sir.*"

"Nothing's come through the gate?"

"*No sir.*"

"Then it's a hive," Ronon said, unfurling like a shadow from where he crouched by the fire. His gaze tipped skyward too. Jack guessed a 'hive' was a ship rather than anything to do with bees.

Pulling his glasses from a pocket as he climbed to his feet, Daniel said, "Question is, what they want? They're not here to feed."

"I rather hope," Beckett said, "we don't find out."

Jack turned to Teyla. "Hey, Obi Wan, can you 'feel' where they are?"

Even in the darkness, Jack could see the distant look on her face. It was more than a little creepy but no one else seemed freaked out. Perhaps telepathy, or whatever this turned out to be, was normal in Pegasus? After a moment, Teyla came back to herself. "It is as I feared. The Wraith are in the vicinity of the Ancient Repository."

"Huh," Jack said, unable to keep the sarcasm out of his voice, "didn't see that coming."

Daniel flashed him a narrow-eyed look and climbed to his feet. "It's *unusual*," he said, then turned to Novak. "So what now? Call for backup?"

"There's no time," Ronon objected, his gaze still on the sky as if he could track the damn 'hive' with the naked eye. "Sheppard doesn't have time." Then he smiled, a mere baring of teeth. "Besides, it's a good night for killing Wraith."

A little hush followed that sentence. The big guy and the Wraith clearly had some history, which was good if it gave him an edge. Bad if it made him reckless.

"I should alert Rodney and John first," Teyla said into the silence, reaching for her radio.

*If they're not dead already*, Jack thought but didn't say out loud. Everyone was probably thinking the same thing anyway. Instead he said, "If they're hiding, radio chatter will give them away."

Her face fell and he got a sudden glimpse of real anguish,

of fear lurking behind her calm exterior. "But if we do not warn them…"

He knew it well, the fear that gripped you when your people were in danger, and he felt a softening toward the woman. "They're not amateurs," he said with a quick glance at Daniel to confirm it. "They'll know if the bad guys are sniffing around."

Teyla pursed her lips, the cool mask settling back into place. "Wraith can be very … stealthy."

"Then we'd better be stealthier." He slid a glance at Ronon. "Right, big guy?"

Ronon's predatory smile returned. "Right."

At which point Colonel Novak stomped around the fire. "No one's going anywhere until I say so." His gaze fixed on Jack. "And you can lose the weapon, Jack."

His fingers tightened around the gunstock in an involuntary response. "You're kidding, right? There are a whole bunch of space-vampires out there, and you still want to bench me?"

"I have my orders—"

"Well screw your orders, Colonel. Things have changed."

A muscle ticked in the guy's jaw, a flash of indecision sparking in his eyes. "General O'Neill—"

"O'Neill can go—" He bit that off hard, changed tack. "Look, *Colonel*, I was commanding spec ops missions when you were still in high school. I literally wrote the SOPs on covert gate operations, and I will not—will *not*—walk into an ambush situation unarmed." He took a step closer, right into the guy's space. "Am I making myself clear?"

Behind Novak, Jack could sense his men stiffen, readying themselves for whatever order the colonel might give. Jack didn't look, kept his gaze locked on Novak's. He seemed like good people, Jack didn't want to hurt the guy, but he was not going to let these people hang him out to dry because they were too chickenshit scared of him to allow him to defend himself.

Daniel cleared his throat. Jack ignored him too.

After a moment, Novak's chin lifted. "Jackson," he said, "give O'Neill your sidearm. Jack—give Dr. Jackson the rifle."

For a beat, two beats, Jack hesitated. It was a compromise, a face-saving compromise and he didn't want to take it. On the other hand, they were off-world with the enemy nearby and Jack had no doubt that O'Neill's orders had included keeping Jack in line by 'any means necessary'. And this wasn't worth dying for.

"Daniel's a crappy shot," Jack said to Novak. "But it's your call, Colonel."

Then he turned to find Daniel watching him with a sober expression. "I'm not a crappy shot," he said as he unholstered his Beretta and held it out to Jack.

It was almost enough to make Jack smile as he took it and gave Daniel the P90 in return. "Sure you are," he said. "Couldn't hit the side of a barn."

Daniel didn't reply, just looked at Jack with enough sympathy to make him turn away. The last thing he needed from Daniel was pity. Making sure the safety was on, he tucked the Beretta into the back of his waistband in lieu of a holster. Across the remains of the fire, Ronon was watching him with an unreadable expression and Jack met it, held it. This guy, Jack thought, understood a lot more than he let on.

Novak had moved away, conferring with Teyla, and a moment later he gave the order to move out. "We'll do a little recon," he said, "before we move in. Ronon, take point. Teyla, stay with him and yell if you sense anything change."

"I don't think yelling would be advisable," she said. "But I will alert you."

And then they were moving, Daniel at Jack's side and the doc on the other, Novak and his men covering their six. It felt wrong to be shepherded into the middle of the formation with the civilians, but he tamped down on the irritation. Worse, to let it distract him. Besides, the cool pressure of the pistol at the small of his back was some comfort. He wouldn't go down without a fight.

Daniel let his mind work as they walked, only slightly disturbed by the prickly aura of resentment radiating from Jack. This man was different from the man he knew, quicker to irritation, less phlegmatic. He wondered if *his* Jack had been more like this when he was younger, whether the youth of his body made him more restless, or whether it was the last ten years of life that had changed him. He suspected the latter. O'Neill and his clone may have been identical when the clone was first created, but Jack was growing into a different man in his own right. Daniel wondered whether he even realized it. For all his protestations that General O'Neill had stolen his life, this younger man was reshaping himself to fit his new one. Daniel just hoped he could make it a good life, one with value and meaning.

But those were questions for another time and he pushed them aside as Ronon led them off the path and into the woods, his Runner's skills making light work of the darkness. The question he needed to answer now was why the Wraith would be interested in the Ancient Repository and, really, there was only one answer: they wanted its knowledge. But how could they access it? He knew that they shared the Ancient's lineage, but he also knew that they couldn't operate Lantean technology, which meant the repository couldn't—wouldn't—download its data into the mind of a Wraith. The obvious solution to that was— "Oh shit."

He didn't realize he'd said it out loud until Jack looked at him. "What?"

"I think I just figured out what the Wraith want." He blew out a breath, glanced ahead to Ronon and Teyla, and lowered his voice. "It's Sheppard."

Jack frowned. "Because... They want what he knows?" He tapped his head. "The Ancient crap?"

"Think about it. It could tell them everything—about Atlantis, its defenses." He swallowed. "About how to reach Earth."

"They don't need Shepherd," Jack pointed out. "They could use anyone with the magic gene, right?"

"Right," Daniel said. "Which means, whatever happens here, we can't let the repository fall into their hands."

Jack's attention shifted back to Ronon and Teyla, weaving through the trees ahead of them. "This Shepard guy is their CO, right?"

"Yeah," Daniel said. "He's a good man."

Jack was silent, boots tramping in the dirt, gaze fixed ahead. "No one gets left behind," he says. "That was always the mantra, right?"

Daniel flicked a look at him. "It still is."

A harsh little smile twitched at the corner of Jack's mouth. "Right. Sure."

Something twanged guiltily in the pit of Daniel's stomach. "Jack, we didn't leave you—"

"Point is, if it comes right down to it, we're gonna have to blow the joint whether or not Shephard's fixed, right?" He turned his gaze on Daniel, eyes a hard glitter in the darkness. "That's what you're saying."

Daniel licked his lips and wondered, briefly, how he'd reached this point. How Daniel Jackson, idealist and humanitarian, had become so pragmatic, so hard-nosed. Somewhere, he supposed, between the Goa'uld murdering his wife, the Replicators threatening to wipe-out the galaxy, and the Ori embarking on holy war. Yeah, that kind of crap will kill a person's idealism. "I'm *saying* we can't let the Ancient Repository fall into the hands of the Wraith. I'm *hoping* we fix Shephard first."

"Right," Jack said, turning his back to Ronon. "Well, here's hoping."

"Don't be an ass," he muttered, irritated despite his better judgment.

"Ha. *I'm* being the ass here?"

"The other you would understand," Daniel said, and regretted the words the moment they left his mouth. "I didn't—" He winced. *Crap.*

After a silence, Jack said, "From what I can tell, the other me has a stick up his ass. Guess that's what happens when you sell your soul to the Pentagon."

"He hasn't—" Daniel took a breath, tamping down on his irritation. "Okay. The point is, Jack, that you and I are a lot less invested in this than the others. We have to keep a clear head. You get that, right?"

After a beat, he said, "What about Novak? He's not a local."

"Yeah well," Daniel said, casting a glance over his shoulder. "I'm sure Novak's a good man, but I don't know him. And, clone or not, when push comes to shove I'd rather have you on my side."

Jack was silent again and then ran a hand through his hair in a gesture that was so familiar, so *Jack*, it actually hurt. Daniel had to look away, swallow a couple times and clear his throat before saying, "You know I've got your back, right? And not just out here. I'm on your side, Jack."

Jack spared him a scant look, then nodded. "Yeah," he said after a moment, his voice a little gruff. "Yeah, okay."

"I mean it," Daniel said. "And not just me. Teal'c, Sam, even General O'Neill, we're all on your side."

Jack didn't reply to that and so they walked on together in silence.

Dawn was a turning the overcast sky gray by the time Ronon slowed them to a halt, dropping to one knee behind the trunk of a large tree. Teyla did the same and Jack crouched low as he moved past Daniel to join them.

"That it?" he asked in a patrol whisper. Ahead of them was a pile of stones, resolving as the light grew into the ruined remains of a building. There were no signs of life, human or otherwise.

Teyla nodded and murmured, "There are Wraith close by, but not many. They are— They are afraid."

"Of what?" Jack said, settling down next to her and peering out through the trees. "Of us?"

"Perhaps." She shook her head, as if puzzling it out. "They are hiding."

Behind them a twig snapped underfoot and Jack turned, reaching for his weapon as Novak approached with a grimace. "Any hostiles?" he said, settling next to Jack.

"Not that we can see. Teyla says they're hiding from something."

Novak ran a hand over his mouth. "Well let's hope it keeps them busy. We don't have time to wait."

"Yeah," Jack said. "We should get in there while it's still mostly dark."

The colonel fixed him with a look, face drawn tight in the subtle morning light. "We can't all go in, we'd risk getting pinned down."

"Yep." Jack glanced back at Daniel and Beckett, at Novak's men keeping a wary eye on the woods. "You should send me, Daniel and the doc inside. The rest of you stay here until you've made the Wraith."

Novak nodded, but without much enthusiasm. "Yeah, I know." He let out a breath, brow furrowing. "My orders…" He didn't finish the sentence. "Okay, we got no choice. We'll cover you on the way in, then set up a perimeter around the structure and secure your egress."

Although he kept it from his face, Jack felt a fierce pulse of satisfaction. At *last*. "Careful, Novak. Almost looks like you're starting to trust me."

"What can I say? Necessity's a mother."

Jack bit back a smile, then turned to Daniel and Beckett. "Doctors? We're going in."

"Wait." Teyla put her hand on his arm. "Ronon and I should go with you." She turned her appeal toward Novak. "John is our friend and teammate."

"And if there's Wraith out here," Novak said, "we need your skill-set here, Teyla." His gaze travelled to encompass Ronon. "Both of you."

Ronon nodded. "Better to hunt Wraith than sit around watching the doc work."

"I don't—" But whatever her objection, Teyla bit down on it and then nodded. "Yes, you are right. Dr. Beckett and Rodney will work better with fewer people holding guns standing about watching them." She visibly straightened her shoulders, and then nodded off to her right. "I am sensing the Wraith in that direction."

Taking that as his cue, Jack rose to his feet, still keeping low. "Daniel, Beckett—get ready."

Daniel was right behind him, but Beckett stopped for a moment to touch Teyla's arm. "I'll bring him back, love," he said. "Don't you worry."

She gave a brief smile. "Thank you. I know that you will. And Carson? Be careful."

"You too," he said, then turned to Jack, chin lifted in the way civilians do when they're trying to look brave. "What are we waiting for?"

With a final glance at Novak, who just nodded his response, Jack turned his eyes on the Ancient structure ahead. It was low, single story, with a wide doorway that opened onto nothing but darkness. Two heavy pillars supported the entrance, and its flat roof butted up against a low rise of land. Jack suspected tunnels of some kind delved into the earth behind it. Pulling the Beretta out of his waistband, he chambered a round and glanced over his shoulder.

"Beckett, stay with me. Daniel, cover our six. Stay low and move as fast as you can until we're under cover."

Both men nodded, Daniel swinging his P90 into his hands and Beckett resettling the weight of the medical pack he was carrying across his shoulders.

"Let's do it," Jack said, and started to run.

The scratchy grassland between them and cover felt twice as long as it looked, conscious as he was of Beckett's heavy footfalls on his heels and the gaze of invisible eyes—imagined or otherwise—peering out from the shadowy trees.

A covey of birds broke from the woods to his right, and he spun, gun lifting as he ran. But there was nothing there—nothing he could see at any rate.

"Crap," Beckett hissed, stumbling. Daniel grabbed his arm and kept him on his feet and moving forward.

Ahead of them the ruins loomed drab against the ashen sky, cold and dank as Jack skidded into the shelter of the portico. He took cover, keeping his weapon on the silent trees as Beckett and Daniel followed him into the gloom, both breathing heavily. He cocked an eyebrow at Daniel, "Too much time behind a desk, Dr. Jackson?"

"Says the twenty-something," Daniel groused.

Beckett smiled, catching his breath. "At least *you* got a younger body out of it, lad," he said. "Count your blessings."

It was a kinda odd statement, and Jack might have questioned it if a horribly familiar voice behind him hadn't chosen that moment to say, "Beckett, is that you?"

The doc turned. "Rodney!"

"Well it's about damn time," McKay said, looming out of the dark doorway. "What took you so long?" His eyes slipped past Jack, to Daniel. "Wait, where's O'Neill? Oh, don't tell me, the cantankerous old bastard wouldn't come. Well, that's typical. I told Teyla that he'd never—"

"Hey," Jack said. "The cantankerous old bastard's right here, McKay. And next time, why don't you whine a little louder? I don't think all the Wraith heard you."

McKay blinked at him. "You're not—" He looked from Jack to Beckett. "What's going on?"

"He's a clone," Beckett said, lifting an eyebrow as if daring McKay to comment.

"Oh. Well, that's—" His attention flipped back to Jack. "Wait a second. Did you say *Wraith*?"

"We think there's a hive in orbit," Daniel explained, with a glance at Jack. "And we think they might be after what's in the Ancient Repository."

McKay snorted. "Like they'd be able to access— Crap. They want Sheppard."

"Got it one," Jack said. "So how about we break up the knitting circle and get on with fixing your guy and getting the hell outa here?"

With only a little more grumbling, Rodney led them further back into the structure. Jack had been right, it definitely delved back into the embankment behind. The tunnels were dark, rock-clad, and reminiscent of a bunker.

"This is old," Daniel murmured as they walked, the beam of his flashlight dancing over the rocks.

"Yeah, genius, it's Ancient," Jack said.

"No, I mean *really* old." Daniel squinted to take a closer look at some of the writings etched into the stone. "Pre-Wraith, obviously."

"Obviously."

"Because otherwise they wouldn't have built it," Daniel explained. "They'd never have put this much information somewhere the Wraith could get hold of—" He broke off as they rounded a corner into a square chamber lit by a few lights flickering in one wall, spiraling out from the familiar shape of the Ancient head-sucking-device.

Jack sighed. "Awesome."

Daniel threw him a look. "*Awesome?*"

"What?"

"You sound like a—" He blinked and shut his mouth. "Okay, never mind."

The scuff of a boot against rock had Jack's gun raised again as a figure emerged from an alcove to the left of the head-sucker. Tall, dark-haired and in uniform, he braced himself against the wall with one hand and said, "Rodney, *comdo asordo*."

McKay's lips tightened. "Sheppard, I told you to rest." He glanced at Beckett. "He keeps trying to wander off. Maybe we should tie him up or something?"

"It's okay," Daniel said, taking a step toward Sheppard, one hand outstretched. "We're here to help you, Colonel." He thought for a moment. "Um, *sumus hic ad asordium vobis*."

Sheppard's gaze swung toward Daniel. "*Possis*?"

"Yes," Daniel nodded. "Yes we can."

With a heave, Beckett swung his pack off and set it on the floor. "How long has he been like this?"

"Sounding like a Latin dictionary?" McKay said. "About twelve hours."

Beckett tutted. "Aye, well, it was to be expected. But we're here now." He glanced up at Jack. "Help me with this, would you?"

From his pack, he was pulling a laptop and what looked like half a roomful of IT hardware. "This is gonna work?" Jack said, doubtful.

"I certainly hope so," Beckett said. "There are two problems, you understand. We can't just delete the data from Colonel Sheppard's brain. Well, we could, but it would delete *all* the data from his brain."

"As in everything," McKay clarified. "Now some might argue that it wouldn't really matter to Sheppard, but we figured he'd still want to know how to use a knife and fork. And, you know, talk."

Jack ignored him. A decade or so might have whitened McKay's hair but it hadn't made him any less irritating. "So what does this do?"

"We need to reconnect Sheppard to the Ancient Repository and get it to reverse the download—to identify its own data and eliminate it from the Colonel's brain. We have no technology capable of that, but the Ancients do. We just need to convince it to do it." He glanced up at Jack. "Which is where you come in."

"By…?"

Beckett shifted where he was crouching next to the device, watching Rodney plug it into the nest of wires that were already attached to the head-sucker. "We need to show it your brain."

"Show it my brain?"

"By wiring you up to this," Beckett said. "Once the Ancient repository has seen what your brain looks like with the data removed, it should be able to identify the same pathways in Colonel Sheppard's brain and then replicate the removal."

Jack glanced at Daniel, who just shrugged, and for a moment he wished profoundly for Carter. She could have explained all this in a way that actually made sense. At the least, he'd have had faith that it might actually work. But Carter wasn't here, she was long gone, and Jack had to do this alone just like he'd done everything else alone for the past decade. "How long will it take?" he said, throwing a glance at the door. They could have company at any moment.

Beckett shook his head. "As long as the proverbial piece of string, I'm afraid. It's not like I've done this before."

Faced now with the prospect of having someone else poking about in his mind, he felt a rising unease that he'd not allowed himself to think about until this point. Coming here had been a way to escape his predicament at the SGC, but now he was in this dank, Ancient shrine with an enemy he'd never even seen waiting in the wings, he was beginning to wonder if he'd jumped out of the frying pan and into a really big fire. He swallowed and it drew Beckett's attention.

"Don't worry, lad," he said with a reassuring smile. "It'll be fine."

Jack wished he could believe him, but too much experience had shown him the lie behind that easy promise. Not that it mattered. "I got no choice anyway," he said, "so let's just get on with this."

Beckett studied him for a moment then gave a curt nod and

started the device booting up, all beeps and flashing lights in the gloom.

Jack turned away, turned right into Daniel who was fixing him with one of those earnest looks he remembered so well. "Daniel…" He sighed. "What?"

"Nothing. Just— Just that you *do* have a choice, Jack. You don't have to do this."

He let his lip curl into a slight smile. "Right. I could walk away and let this guy die."

"You could," Daniel pressed. "You could have said no in the first place."

He shook his head, held Daniel's gaze. "Come on, we both know that's not true. That's not my life, Daniel. I'm not that guy anymore."

"You still have a *choice*," Daniel insisted. "You're no one's tool, here, Jack."

Easy to say. He glanced over at Sheppard, who still stood by the far wall, gazing at them through blank eyes. He wondered if this is how he'd looked when his mind was being overwritten, detached and lost and *alien*. "I guess I choose to save this guy's life, then," he said, and threw Daniel a relenting look. "Beats dying in front of the TV."

"Right," Daniel said, although he narrowed his eyes and looked unconvinced. "It's not going to end here, Jack. I mean that. I didn't bring you here to die saving Sheppard."

He smiled at that, all smoked-glass and deflection. "From your lips to the false-gods' ears, Daniel."

# CHAPTER FIVE

"WE NEED to give you a sedative," Beckett said. "Before we hook you up to the device."

Glancing up at Daniel from where he lay on a bedroll on the floor, Jack said, "Guess that puts you in charge."

"Pretty sure I already was."

Almost, Jack smiled at that. Instead, he nodded toward the doorway as Becket pulled up his sleeve and prepared the shot. "Keep an eye open for visitors."

Daniel nodded as Beckett said "Just a scratch on your arm… There. Now count backward from five for me…"

"Five," Jack said, "four." He blinked heavily, sinking down into the dark. "Three…"

And then a radio crackled to life, voice spitting out. *"Incoming—"*

He fought his way back up, but everything was heavy, dark and—

*And something grips his head like a vice, an enormous pressure—invasive, cold, ruthless. His brain is pushing out from the inside of his skull, he can feel synapses snap, bone fracture, a blaze of white light across his eyes.*

*Dimly, someone's yelling.*

*He thinks it might be Daniel.*

*Words slosh around, incomprehensible, but he can feel the cold floor beneath him, the tear of a scream in his throat. Hands on his arms, desperate, pulling at him.*

*And then a detonation, a shadow. Then darkness.*

"Get back!" McKay hissed, grabbing Daniel's arm and yanking him around the corner into the narrow, dirt tunnel. "They'll see you."

Loam, worms, damp: it clogged Daniel's nose, his heaving

chest. He almost gagged on it. Or maybe it was on the fear and anger and guilt. "We can't leave him in there!"

"And how do you think charging back in is going to help?" McKay grimaced and slid down the wall into a crouch. "There must have been a dozen Wraith in there."

"I counted three."

"Yeah, well, they were big. And—" McKay grimaced, shifting position, and Daniel noticed he was holding his right arm, hugging it to his chest.

"You're hurt." He hadn't even noticed in the panic to get out—to get Jack out—when the Wraith attacked. "Let me see."

"Nothing to look at," McKay said, his jaw tight. "A stunner must have clipped me. My whole arm's numb. It'll wear off in a couple hours. Assuming we're not dead already."

Letting out a breath, Daniel came to crouch next to him, his back to the dirt tunnel's wall. "Where does this even go?" He daren't use the flashlight on his weapon, but couldn't see far in the scant light filtering back from the Repository room. "Can we get out?"

"Maybe," McKay said with a grimace. "The place is a rabbit warren, and I mean that almost literally."

"If we could get back to Teyla and the others…"

"Assuming they're still alive. No one's answering their radio."

Daniel didn't comment on that. There were plenty of reasons that could explain it—the small mountain of dirt over their heads, for one. "Let's just stay positive, McKay."

"Well, I'm sorry, Pollyanna, but I'm not seeing a lot of positives in our current situation."

Daniel let his head knock back against the wall, tried and failed not to picture the sudden, shocking, carnage that had overtaken them: Beckett slumped in a corner, unconscious; Jack writhing in pain as the Ancient device took hold of his mind; the Wraith driving McKay and Daniel into the tunnels. McKay was right, there weren't a lot of positives. "We're not dead," he said at last. "There's that."

McKay tutted and fussed with his injured arm. "That's setting a pretty low bar."

Daniel couldn't deny he had a point.

Jack woke to a scene straight out of a horror movie. A monstrous face loomed above him, all fangs and yellow eyes, skin like ash, and claws on its massive hands. "Sonofa—" He scrambled backward, heart pounding, trying to figure out what the hell was going on. The thing cocked its head, studying him, flexing its clawed hand. "Hey," Jack said. "What's up?"

If it understood him, the creature—he was assuming 'Wraith'—didn't respond. It did, however, stand up and turn away with a swirl of its long, leather coat to go and inspect the head-sucking device.

*Space-vampire-Goths?* "And I thought the Goa'uld were ostentatious."

A soft groan came from somewhere behind him and he turned to see Beckett groggily sitting up. "Are you okay?" he said, as soon as he saw Jack watching.

"Better than you," Jack said, shuffling back toward him. "What happened?"

Beckett flexed his hands like they were numb, and then rubbed at his head. "They burst in just after I'd administered the sedative. Colonel Novak tried to warn us, but— I don't know what's happened outside. His radio communication cut off, and then I must have been hit by a stunner." He grimaced and flexed his hands again. "At close range, I think."

Jack's eyes moved to the weapon holstered at the Wraith's side. "Non-lethal?"

Beckett gave a grim smile. "They like their food fresh."

"Peachy." He glanced around the room again with a beat of sudden alarm. "Where's Sheppard? Did Fangs over there take him?"

Beckett shook his head. "I don't know. Last thing I saw, the colonel was putting up a good fight."

The Wraith turned suddenly, moving away from the head-sucker as if he'd been summoned, and taking a couple of steps toward the door. He was met there with another Wraith, equally ugly and over-dressed, and for a moment they just stood staring at each other.

"What's that?" Jack asked Beckett under his breath. "Some kinda chick-flick moment?"

"They can communicate telepathically," Beckett said. "Believe me, Jack, there's nothing chick-flick about the Wraith."

"You know something about these guys, huh?"

"Aye, something. I, um, lived with them for a while—in a way."

Perhaps they'd heard him, or perhaps they'd just finished their staring contest, but at that moment both Wraith turned and fixed their alien eyes on Jack. "You speak Lantean—the language of the Ancestors?" Fangs said.

"Um, sure. Mostly tourist Lantean. 'How much is a beer?' 'Which way's the beach?' That kinda thing."

"We seek—" He stopped, turned to his friend and had another silent conversation—an argument, maybe—before turning back to Jack. "We seek your assistance."

Jack let his eyebrows climb. "And I should help you, because?"

The Wraith's expression didn't change, he remained as cool and utterly alien as before. "Because otherwise," he said, "we will feed on you and on your friends. Including the two hiding in the tunnel. And the five in the woods that surround this place."

"That sounds like a threat. I don't respond well to threats."

From behind him, Beckett murmured, "Perhaps we should find out what it is they want?"

"That's a good point." Jack fixed his gaze on the Wraith. "Because if it's fashion advice, I can tell you that leather is so last season."

The Wraith took a step forward. "Your words meaning nothing to me, human. I require you to speak with the Lantean who has accessed the Ancestor's library. There is knowledge within it that we seek."

"I bet there is."

"You will assist us in retrieving it."

"Yeah. You know what? Bite me."

The Wraith bared its teeth. "If you wish."

Beckett put a quelling hand on Jack's shoulder. "What information is it you're after?" he said to the Wraith. "There might be a compromise to be reached."

Turning its baleful glare on the doc, Fangs said, "One of our number is…"

Again, he turned back to the Wraith who stood behind him, half hidden in the shadows of the corridor. Again, that silent conversation. Debate, perhaps? But whatever they were discussing, Fangs had obviously won because the other Wraith turned and disappeared back into the darkness.

After a pause, the Wraith turned back around to face them. "Our child is sick," he said. "We believe the cure can be found in the works of the Ancestors. But," and here his face twisted in an expression of disdain that was devastatingly human, "the Ancestors chose to lock their knowledge away from us, their children, and so we must resort to … *threats* to retrieve what we seek."

On his shoulder, Jack felt Beckett's hand tighten. "Well," he said, "as it happens I'm a doctor. A healer. Perhaps I could look at your little one and see what I can do?"

"In exchange," Jack said, before the good doc got too carried away, "for the release of our people. Naturally."

"Our masters of science biological could not help her," the Wraith said, disdain ripe in his voice. "The problem is beyond your understanding, human. It involves the sequencing of …" he hesitated, perhaps looking for the right word, "… of a specific group of bonded atoms within her body."

Beckett sat up a little straighter. "Which group?"

"You would not understand—"

"Why don't you give it a try?" Beckett said. "Describe its function."

The Wraith hesitated again, then said, "It is responsible for replication within the body."

Beckett clicked his fingers. "That's what I thought. We call it deoxyribonucleic acid." He glanced at Jack. "That's DNA."

"Sure," he said with a sage nod. "I knew that."

Beckett scrambled to his feet, although his legs still looked somewhat wobbly from the effects of the stunner and he had to brace a hand against the wall. "As it happens," he said, "I've become something of an expert on DNA sequencing—both human and Wraith. Why don't you let me look at the child?"

In the corridor beyond, there was sound, a slight movement of shadow, and a small pale face peered out of the dark: the Wraith child, a girl by the look of the dress she wore. The Wraith turned in alarm when he saw her there, holding out a warning hand. "Stay back," he said. "Where is Balm?"

"With the Lantean," the child said, and then coughed, her hand pressed to her middle.

"You should be resting."

"Balm sent me to find you. The Lantean sleeps and won't wake up."

Jack hissed a curse through his teeth and scrambled to his feet. "We're running out of time," he said. "Look, Fangs, you gotta let us help our guy. He's *dying*."

"Then you are right," the Wraith snarled, raising its weapon. "We are running out of time."

Jack took a step forward, put himself between the Wraith and Beckett. "That's not gonna help. The doc here is your best shot. Let him look at your kid, let him see if there's something he can do, but in the meantime you gotta let him finish what he started here— Let us help Sheppard and then we'll help your kid."

The Wraith's stunner didn't move, still leveled at Jack. "You will speak with the Lantean, you will ask him our questions. You will ask him—"

"He won't have the answers to your questions!" Jack snapped. "Trust me, I know. That thing is rewiring his brain. It's *killing* him. He's not a one-man Wikipedia, he *can't help you.*"

The Wraith's weapon didn't waver, but an expression like doubt skittered across its face. "He was our last hope. You will ask the questions—"

"I can't. Even if I could, it wouldn't help. This isn't your solution. I'm sorry." And he was, he realized. As freakishly alien as this creature looked, he was a father in pain and Jack understood that. Cliché or not, it was a pain he wouldn't wish on his worst enemy.

Behind him, Beckett cleared his throat. "And there's nothing more your own people can do for her? Your scientists are—"

"My *people*," the Wraith spat, "are as indifferent as the Ancestors to the fate of my child."

And now *that*, Jack thought, was odd. "They brought you here, didn't they?" he said, fishing. "In your 'hive' ship up there?"

This time, the Wraith did lower his weapon, his face tipping up to the ceiling in alarm. "There is a hive in orbit?" You didn't need to be an expert in Wraith to see the stark fear on its face.

"Well, we assumed…" Jack traded a bemused look with Beckett who just lifted his shoulders in a shrug. "Where the hell did you come from if it wasn't a hive? It wasn't through the gate."

The Wraith slumped, perhaps in relief or maybe just in despair. "We have a small cruiser. We are— We left the hive to come here and we cannot return. This place was our last hope."

"It still can be," Jack said, taking a step forward, keeping one eye on the Wraith's weapon. He wondered how hard it would be to wrest the thing from the creature's grip. "Look, I know what it's like to be cast out. To have nowhere to turn, no friends to back you up. It sucks, I get that. But the doc here, he's pretty smart. And back on Atlantis they've got all kinds of gizmos, right doc?"

He glanced behind him to see Beckett watching him with controlled alarm. "Aye," he said, cautiously, "but—"

"See?" Jack turned back to the Wraith, ignoring Beckett's concern. "This isn't the end of the road. We can *help* you. You just have to let us help our friend first."

"And why should I trust you, Lantean? The people of Atlantis are no friends to the Wraith."

Jack shrugged. "Maybe not," he said, "but I'm not from Atlantis. I'm not from anywhere. Like you, I'm all on my own out here. So I guess we'll just have to trust each other." He held out his hands, palms up. "It's not like either of us have much choice."

The Wraith held Jack's gaze for a long, long moment, his eyes unblinking reptilian slits of color in his grey face. And then he turned back to the child hovering in the shadows and the stunner dipped, his fingers loosening on the weapon. Jack flexed his fingers, wondered whether to grab for it, but figured trust was more important than firepower at this point. "If I agree," the Wraith said, "it is Creation's life I am putting in your hands. Without her, my own is meaningless."

"I understand," Jack said. "We'll do the best we can for her, I swear. Once we've got Sheppard back, we'll do everything we can to save her." Behind him, Beckett was shuffling his feet, no doubt uncomfortable with Jack's promise. It was a promise he had no authority to make, he knew. "You have *my* word," he said, holding out his hand. "I'll do everything I can to help your kid."

The Wraith stared at his hand then extended his own, his

left instead of his right, which made for an odd handshake, but what the heck. A deal was a deal.

"Cool," Jack said. "Now let's get to work."

It turned out the Ancient Repository did have a back door, an extremely overgrown, heavy back door. And it opened with a screech that Daniel felt down into his bones, piercing the silence of the tunnels.

There was no way on Earth that the Wraith hadn't heard it.

"Run," he growled, crowding McKay out through the narrow gap ahead of him. "Head for the trees."

"Oh, great plan," McKay grumbled, even as he started to sprint. "We're in a *forest!*"

Ignoring him, Daniel wrenched his P90 after him through the doorway and sprinted for the thicker tree-line just ahead. It had been dawn when they entered the repository, and it was now well past noon. The planet's fat sun sent lengthening shadows through the woods, stripes of darkness and light, and Daniel dropped to a crouch in a patch of dense shade, hiding behind a tree as he caught his breath and watched the tunnel entrance. From this angle he could see the side of the structure rising up through the undergrowth, its carved stone worn and chipped by the elements, the back end of the building disappearing into the steep bank behind him.

McKay was a couple dozen feet past him, deeper into the trees, but Daniel could still hear his heavy, panicked breathing. "There could be hundreds of them out here," he hissed. "We have to keep moving."

Daniel just held up a hand to quiet him, listening. There was nothing, no slap of booted feet, no orders shouted. Nothing to suggest they were being followed. Which was … odd. The Wraith had sharp hearing, there was no way they could have missed the sound of that door opening.

"Jackson," McKay hissed. "We have to move."

Turning, treading as silently as he could, Daniel made his

way over to McKay. "I don't think anyone's following us."

"Yet."

"No, listen." They listened, but the only sounds were the chatter of birds, the whisper of a breeze through the treetops. "Nothing."

McKay blinked at him, looked around with a frown. "You're right," he said. "That's… Probably bad. It's always bad."

Ignoring McKay's reflexive pessimism, Daniel said, "We should head back to our last position, see if we can regroup with the others." But his gaze travelled back to the repository, now in the hands of the Wraith, and beyond that back to his conversation with Jack. They couldn't let the repository fall into Wraith hands, which meant that, unless Jack and the others could overwhelm the Wraith, they were going to have to destroy the structure—no matter who was left inside.

He just hoped that Novak would be willing to give the order, and that Ronon and Teyla would obey it if he did. "Come on," he said to McKay. "We don't have much time."

The process wasn't quick, which Jack supposed was unsurprising.

Sheppard lay flat on the stone floor, his head wired up to the device that Beckett had brought with him, while Beckett crouched next to him, his gaze darting from the laptop to Sheppard and then up to the head-sucking device that was trailing cables across the floor. Jack watched them both from his place a couple feet away, back propped against the wall. His part in this was done and the only thing left was a muzzy sensation in his head—like his brain had been taken out, shaken around, and put back in place. Which, he guessed, it kinda had.

He glanced at his watch and wondered where Daniel and McKay had gotten to. The Wraith had said they were hiding in the tunnels, and if that was true then Jack was pretty sure they wouldn't stay hidden for long. Daniel had never been good at keeping his head down, and he doubted a decade had made a lot of difference. Putting himself on the line for others was pretty much what Daniel did, which meant they didn't have a lot of time before he made his move, and that could get nasty. He'd really prefer Sheppard on his feet by then.

"Is it working?" he asked Beckett, not for the first time.

Beckett flicked him a glance, just shy of irritated. "Aye. I think so. But it'll take time, this is a delicate process."

Jack just nodded, schooled himself to patience, and let his gaze drift over to the Wraith who were camped out by the doorway. Deal or not, there was no doubt about who was wearing the pants here. Fangs—the one Jack had spoken with—was obviously on guard, while the other Wraith sat on the floor with the kid. She lay sleeping, curled up on the ground, and the Wraith rested a protective hand on her head. It was such a human gesture, his hand to her head, that it made Jack's palm tingle with sense memory of soft hair, a child's warmth. He had to look away.

He shifted and Beckett glanced up, a question in his narrowing eyes.

Jack had no desire to answer it, so instead he quietly said, "You really think you can help the kid?"

The doc's lips tightened and he looked over at her, then back to Jack. "I hope so. Like I said, I know a few things about Wraith DNA."

"Yeah." Jack watched him for a moment, caught the half-smothered expression on his face that hinted at truths unspoken, and remembered Beckett's odd, wistful conversation with Daniel about turnips. "So what's the deal?" Jack said. "With you and the Wraith."

Beckett looked down at the laptop again, then over at Sheppard. "Me and the Wraith?"

"You said you'd lived with them for a while."

"So I did."

"I'm assuming it wasn't an exchange program..."

Beckett's mouth twisted into what might have been a smile.

"In a way it was." He lifted his eyes to Jack and held his gaze for a long, measured beat. "I didn't know whether to tell you this, but perhaps…" He gave a little shrug. "Carson Beckett died several years ago. I'm his clone, created by the Wraith."

Jack stared, incredulous. "You're a— *What*?"

Beckett huffed a laugh. "Did you think you were the only one, lad?"

"I— Well, kinda. You were created by the *Wraith*?"

He made an equivocal gesture. "Essentially, yes. Not that I knew it at first, of course. It, uh, came as something of a shock."

"Yeah," Jack growled. "I know the feeling." He drummed his fingers on his knee, propped up in front of him. "How did you—?" He shook his head and fell silent. There were a million questions he wanted to ask, but they were all swirling around together and he couldn't make sense of them. "The, uh, the real you is dead?" he said at length.

Beckett gave him a sharp smile. "I like to think of myself as the *real* me," he said. "But, yes, the original Carson Beckett died on Atlantis before I was freed from the Wraith." His gaze dipped back to his patient. "Which is why I can never go home, of course."

"I'm sorry," Jack said, because he knew exactly how much that sucked.

"What for?" Beckett sounded genuinely surprised. "He's dead, I'm not. I'd say I got the best end of the deal."

"Really?" Jack said, shifting uncomfortably. "But you've lost everything—your friends, your family. Your home. Don't you—? Doesn't that make you angry?"

"No." Beckett sat up straighter. "Why should it?"

"Because it was your life—and now it isn't."

Beckett frowned, thoughtful for a moment before he said, "Listen, you can't think like that, lad. It'll eat you up, all that resentment."

"But—"

"*This* is my life," he said. "Here in Pegasus. These are my friends, my family, and Atlantis is my home. Carson had his life and I have mine. I'm not *him*, Jack. My story's not his story. I don't begrudge him his life and I doubt he'd have begrudged me mine." He tipped his head to the side, eyes narrowing. "I doubt General O'Neill begrudges you yours, either, despite the fact that you've got an extra couple of decades and a second chance at life."

It wasn't something that he'd ever considered, that O'Neill might envy *him*. Why would he, when he had everything Jack wanted? But on the far side of the room the Wraith shifted where he sat with his hand on the child's head and Jack felt a flare of something bright, like hope. *He doesn't have everything*, a voice whispered in the back of his mind. *He doesn't have everything you want.*

It was dangerous, that voice, that hope. It was subversive. It felt too much like giving in.

"You're a young man again," Beckett went on, "with the wisdom of a lifetime's experience. There are people who'd trade their soul to be in your position. You should make the most of it."

His gaze still locked on the sleeping child Jack tried to swallow the hopeful burn in his chest. "They left me behind," he said, touching base with his familiar hurt. "They just walked away from me."

"And?"

"And this feels like letting them off the hook."

Beckett gave a wry smile and turned his attention back to his laptop. "Maybe it's letting *you* off the hook, lad. You ever think of that?"

He hadn't. He didn't want to. He'd been angry for ten years and it kept him sharp, kept him breathing. He wasn't sure he knew how to stop.

As it turned out, it wasn't difficult to find the rest of their team; they'd been herded into the clearing in front of the

Ancient repository and were being held there by two Wraith, prowling in nervous circles around Ronon, Teyla, and Novak and his team. Ronon was sprawled on his back, like he'd been dragged there, and Telya sat near him with one hand resting on his shoulder. A couple of Novak's men looked like they were nursing the aftereffects of stunner blasts, but otherwise everyone was in one piece.

"Now what?" McKay hissed where he crouched next to Daniel in the shadows of the trees.

Daniel didn't answer right away, thinking as he glanced around the empty clearing. "I thought there'd be more of them," he said after a pause. "More Wraith."

"What? That's not enough?"

"No darts," Daniel said. "No drones." He squinted up at the white clouds as if he could peer through them and see the hive. "Doesn't it strike you as odd?"

McKay shifted where he crouched. "What's your point?"

"I don't know, exactly. Just— Sometimes things aren't what they seem."

"It *seems* like my team have been captured by the Wraith," McKay pointed out. "It *seems* like we are in deep trouble."

Daniel looked at him over the tops of his glasses. "There's two of them, two of us. Doesn't seem like deep trouble to me." He unsaftied his weapon. "You got a better idea?"

"Go back to the gate, get—"

"Sheppard could be dead by then," Daniel said. "There's no time."

"Well we can't just charge them. We won't stand a chance."

Daniel glanced back at the captured team. Between them, there'd be enough force to overwhelm the Wraith. They just needed a distraction. "How about we surrender?"

"What?"

"Fake-surrender, until we're close enough to rush them. Teyla and the others will join in once we start."

McKay huffed out a breath.

"C'mon, there aren't any other Wraith around. We can do this, McKay."

"Fine. But if I die out there, I'm coming back to haunt you."

Daniel pushed to his feet. "Neither of us believes in ghosts, McKay."

"In principle," he said, following suit.

Daniel allowed himself a small smile, then dropped his weapon and let it hang from his tac vest. "Okay, hands up. I'll do the talking. Just follow my lead."

"I'll be right behind you," McKay said. Then, more quietly, "Like, twenty feet behind you."

Daniel ignored that, took a breath and braced himself before stepping out from cover, hands up. "Hey," he called, getting the Wraith's attention. They both spun to face him, weapons raised. "You missed a couple of us."

He started walking across the clearing, arms up, gun heavy against his chest. Teyla's head shot up. She was already in a low crouch, one hand braced on Ronon's shoulder. Novak moved too, slow enough not to draw attention.

"My name's Daniel Jackson," Daniel said, to fill time and silence, to keep the Wraith's attention. "This is Dr. McKay. We just want to talk."

One of the Wraith hissed, "Stay where you are," while the other turned to cover the rest of the tree-line like they were expecting Daniel to have backup. It only added to the strangeness of their being so few of them. In Daniel's experience, Wraith always attacked in numbers.

"We'd like to negotiate," Daniel said, still walking despite the Wraith's demand for him to stop. "We don't want to fight."

"I said stay where you are!" The Wraith was getting itchy, his hand flexing on the stunner. Daniel figured he had no more than a few seconds before the creature fired.

"Okay," he said, slowing-up but still moving, still edging closer. Behind him he could hear McKay's footsteps, his quick breaths. "Okay, I'll stop," he said, in the same moment he snatched up his weapon and squeezed the trigger.

He got off a short burst, hitting the Wraith's arm and knocking it back and up so the stunner shot went wide. Then he dived to the ground, getting a face full of dirt as the second Wraith opened fire. Rolling to his feet, he saw Teyla pounce on the Wraith Daniel had hit, wrenching the stunner from its injured hand and firing two shots in quick succession.

It went down in a burst of blue energy at the same moment Novak and one of his men barreled into the second Wraith, forcing it to the ground. Daniel scrambled to his feet, McKay still behind him, as Teyla stepped neatly over Ronon's comatose body and fired two more shots into the downed Wraith.

It twitched and lay silent.

"Well," Teyla said, turning to Daniel and McKay with a thin smile. "It is good to see you both." Her gaze slipped toward the repository behind them. "The others?"

Daniel nodded. "Still in there, but there's only a couple Wraith inside." He ventured a smile of his own. "And there's a back door…"

"Then I think it is time to get our people back."

"And destroy the repository," Daniel said, casting a glance at Novak.

"Those aren't our orders, Dr. Jackson," the colonel said, moving back from where his men were tying up the unconscious Wraith.

"We didn't know there'd be Wraith here when we left Atlantis. And we can't let them get access to the Ancient database." He cocked his head. "You know that, right?"

Novak looked uncomfortable, scratched a hand through his dark hair. "We'll blow the joint before we leave," he agreed.

Daniel looked again at Teyla who met his eyes with a cool gaze. "That means even if Beckett's cure didn't work," he said. "Even if Shephard's still…"

Teyla didn't reply, just turned to kneel next to Ronon who was stirring groggily. She put a hand on his arm to sooth him and said, "You would do the same if it was your Jack O'Neill instead of John?"

And that wasn't difficult to answer, even if the memory was painful. "We did," he said quietly. "Jack gave himself up to save Earth and we let him do it. I think Sheppard would want the same."

"He would," Teyla said, helping Ronon to sit. "But let us hope that he will not need to."

"Yeah, let's hope."

Over her head he met Novak's somber gaze. "Our gear's in the trees," the colonel said. "We'll go get the C4 and then you can show us the back door, Dr. Jackson."

The kid sat up with a gasp, one hand pressed to her head. For all that she wasn't human, there was something vulnerable about her that clutched at the tender spot in Jack's chest. Her distress brought Jack up into a low crouch, just as it drew the Wraith by the door to its knees in front of her.

"They are coming," the girl said, face scrunched up in pain. "They are here!"

The two adult Wraith exchanged a silent look, then one of them picked the child up while the other turned its weapon on Jack. "We must leave now. You will come with us."

"No," Beckett said, from where he was kneeling over Sheppard. "It's almost finished, but if I stop now it could kill him."

Arms held out, palms up, Jack got to his feet. "What's happening?" he said, slow and easy.

"Our hive has entered orbit," the Wraith said. "Creation can sense the presence of our Queen. And she— She will know that Creation still lives." He stepped forward, his presence overwhelming in the small room. "There is no more time. You will come with us. Now. We must leave."

"No," Beckett repeated, and Jack took a step sideways, putting himself between the doctor and the wraith.

"Your hive is looking for the kid?"

"Yes. Our queen wishes her dead."

Beckett glanced up. "They want a future queen, dead?"

"She is— In their eyes, Creation is an abomination."

"Because she's sick?"

The Wraith exchanged a look with its colleague, friend—whatever they were. "No," he said. "Because she was created by clevermen, not born of a queen."

Jack felt his eyes go wide. "She's uh…" He glanced back at the doc, who was frowning at the child. "A test-tube baby?"

"Something like that," Beckett said quietly, his gaze fixed on the Wraith. "She's a clone, isn't she? And that's why she's sick. She's suffering from some kind of abnormal gene expression."

The Wraith tipped its head, a gesture at once alien yet understandable. "We do not have time to discuss this now. They will find us and kill us all if we do not leave."

From behind the room, far back in the structure, Jack heard a soft metallic boom. A door slamming, perhaps? If this place had doors. He turned to look, but only the black mouth of the corridor leaving the chamber showed itself. "Sounds like we have company."

In a panic, the wraith spun toward the tunnel, the other one holding the child close as it followed. It didn't get far.

A familiar voice said, "Don't give me an excuse to shoot," and the Wraith were forced back into the room. Ronon followed, his expression set and his weapon levelled and ready. Teyla was at his shoulder and McKay a couple steps behind.

The Wraith snarled, its weapon swinging between Jack and Ronon.

"Wait!" Jack said as behind him he heard a scuffing footstep. He spun around to see Daniel and Novak emerging from the dark, weapons drawn. He flung up a hand. "Wait!"

Daniel's quick gaze darted about the room, taking everything in. "What's going on, Jack?"

"Just— wait. It's not what it looks like."

"Looks like Wraith," Ronon growled.

"They need our help," Jack said at the same moment Teyla said, "There's a child."

Jack sucked in a breath, the only sound in the suddenly silent room. The Wraith, all two of them, were outnumbered and he knew the obvious thing—perhaps the *right* thing—to do was to take them out, grab Sheppard, and get the hell outa dodge before the rest of the Wraith showed up.

But he'd given his word and, besides, he knew too well what it was like when no one had your back—when the people you thought were your friends walked away. And he wouldn't do that. He couldn't.

"There's more wraith on the way," he said. "The hive has shown up looking for these guys. We have to leave now."

Ronon bared his teeth. "Got no argument from me."

"And they're coming with us. I promised we'd help them."

"You don't have that authority," Novak said from behind him, the words sharp with irritation.

"The kid's sick. Beckett can help her."

"*May* be able to help her," Beckett said, from where he crouched next to Sheppard. He had one hand on the man's forehead. "And we can't leave now. Sheppard's starting to wake up. I need another few minutes."

"We can—" Jack began, but his words were cut off by an odd, high pitched whine drifting in from outside. Like a supercharged mosquito or—

"Darts," Teyla said twisting around just as the kid started screaming, clutching at her head.

The Wraith spun back to Jack. "They're here," he hissed. "It's too late. And now we will all die."

"Not on my watch," Jack growled. "Daniel. Back door?"

He nodded. "It'll take us into the woods."

Jack turned back to the Wraith and nodded toward Sheppard. His eyelids were fluttering, but he was still out for the count. "You're strong, right? Can you carry him?"

The Wraith's expression, alien and impassive, didn't change, but he said, "I can."

"That's not—" Beckett began, but cut off when Jack glared. "Okay. I guess it'll have to be long enough," and he started pulling plugs on the laptop.

"Novak, you carrying C4?"

The colonel opened his mouth to say something—to object to Jack taking command, probably—but thought better of it and just said, "Get 'em outa here, Jack. We'll rig the place to blow and see how many Wraith we can take with it."

But Jack shook his head. "They're your people. You get 'em out. I'll blow the joint."

"What?" Daniel lowered his weapon. "Jack—"

"We got no choice."

"Then I'm staying too."

"No. Daniel, get back to the gate."

"You can't—"

"There's no time for a goddamn debate! Novak, get them outa here."

But Daniel grabbed Jack's arm. "I know what you're doing," he said in a low voice. "And just— *Don't*."

"What?"

"You're not planning on coming back, are you?"

Jack glanced at Beckett, but the doc didn't meet his eye. He was still fussing over Sheppard, detaching him from the repository. "I'm coming back," Jack said. "I'm— I don't plan on dying here, Daniel."

For a long beat, Daniel held his gaze, and then he loosened his grip on Jack's arm. "Make sure you don't."

"I'll see you at the gate. Hold it open for me."

Daniel just nodded, brow scrunched.

Jack wasn't sure whether Daniel believed him or not, but he valued his trust anyway. "Novak," he said, hands out. "Gimme the C4 and get these people moving."

# CHAPTER SIX

GENERAL Jack O'Neill stood in the briefing room at Stargate Command, gazing out over the silent gate room. It was late and he should have hit the sack a couple hours ago, but sleep never came easy at the best of times and when he had something on his mind… Well, the silent corridors of the SGC had been his pacing ground for years. No reason to stop now.

He was rarely troubled by indecision or second-guessing, but Coolidge's visit had troubled him. Whatever the rights and wrongs had been of the initial decision to cut the kid—his clone—loose, the fact was that he needed a different solution now. One they could all live with. And by 'all' he had to include the IOA. And that was pretty much impossible, because there was no version of Jack O'Neill who would be happy playing lab rat at Area 51 or performing in the Committee's flee circus.

No. Truth was, he had a choice: do the right thing and face the music, or do the wrong thing and cover his ass.

Jack O'Neill had never been one for CYOA.

Question was: how to do the right thing without bringing everyone else down in the aftermath? Carter and Daniel were already implicated in pulling the kid out of Syria and getting him off-world, and if Jack was to do anything else it wouldn't only be *his* career the IOA would flush. And he couldn't do that to his team.

"O'Neill."

Teal'c's quiet voice startled him, but he hid his surprise with a smile as he glanced over his shoulder. "Hey," he said, glancing at his watch. "Can't sleep?"

"My body is attuned to Dakara," Teal'c said, walking over from the top of the stairs, "where it is currently mid-afternoon."

"Ah, gate-lag," Jack said, turning back to his vigil. "Well, I'm on DC time, so…"

"That is only two hours different, O'Neill."

"It's an important two hours."

Teal'c didn't comment, just came to stand next to Jack, arms folded behind his back as he gazed down that the Stargate. "You are concerned about your clone?"

"What gave me away?"

"It has always been in your nature, O'Neill, to worry about those for whom you believe yourself responsible." He turned to regard Jack with his ageless gaze. "Even when you are not."

Jack let out a breath. "Well, in this case I *am*. Kinda comes with the big desk, Teal'c."

"The clone is an adult, capable of making his own choices."

"But that's the problem, isn't it? He doesn't have any choices. Not really."

Teal'c was silent, regarding Jack for a couple more beats before turning his gaze back on the Stargate. "A man unable to control his own destiny is a slave."

"Right."

"He must fight for his freedom."

Jack let out a slow breath. "It's not always that easy, Teal'c. You know that."

"No, it is not easy. Little worth doing is *easy*." After another silence, Teal'c said, "The day you and I first met, O'Neill, you opened a door for me. You gave me a choice and I took it. Can you not do the same for the clone?"

Jack huffed out a laugh. "Back then I was a colonel, Teal'c, in command of a four-person gate team. Now… There's a lot more at stake, buddy."

"The right decision is still the right decision, despite what is at stake."

And damn him for being right. Jack kicked the toe of his boot against the wall. "Yeah," he sighed. "I know."

"And you have a plan." Teal'c moved, turning so that his back was to the Stargate and he was facing Jack. His expression was shrewd in the way Teal'c often was, without flamboyance, just *knowing.* "That is why you are here."

"Of a sort," Jack said, permitting a slight smile. "How well you know me, T."

"Indeed."

"It's gonna put Carter and Daniel in the firing line. Carter mostly, I guess."

Teal'c tipped his head with a slight frown. "That will not concern them."

"Oh, I know that," Jack said. "But it concerns *me*."

After a moment's consideration, Teal'c said, "Because you feel this situation is of your making?"

He hadn't exactly considered it like that, but Teal'c always did have a knack of hitting the proverbial nail on its proverbial head. "I guess so. And because the kid—the clone—is me. This feels like my mess to clean up."

"O'Neill." Teal'c put a hand on his shoulder, fingers digging into his muscle. "Are we not family after all these years? You would not ask anything of them that they would not willingly offer, nor ask of you in return."

For a long beat Jack held Teal'c's steady gaze, then he nodded. "Yeah," he said as Teal'c let go. "Yeah, you're right." He sucked in a breath, took a last look at the Stargate, and said, "C'mon, I need to find Harriman. I've got a message to send to the *Hammond*."

Sheppard came round half way back to the gate, kneed the Wraith carrying him slung over one shoulder in the chest, and sent them both crashing down into the dirt.

"No!" Daniel yelled, sliding to a halt and scrambling to get back to them before someone got hurt.

Above, the sky was alive with Wraith darts and the team was strung out in a ragged line under cover of the trees. It was dark, but he wasn't entirely sure that didn't give the Wraith an advantage; they preferred to attack at night.

Wild, disoriented, Sheppard fought himself free of the

Wraith and dropped into a low crouch, arms raised to fight. "What the—?"

"John, it's alright!" Teyla darted past Daniel, almost barreling into Sheppard. Putting herself between him and the Wraith, arms spread wide. "Do not hurt him!"

The Wraith was back on his feet, stunner in his hand. He looked pissed.

"Teyla?" Sheppard shook his head, disoriented. "What's going on?"

"There is no time to explain," Teyla said. "We are retreating to the Stargate and there are Wraith in pursuit."

Sheppard pointed a shaky hand at the Wraith who'd been carrying him. "There are Wraith *here*."

"They're on our side," Daniel said, taking a step closer. "For now, at least."

The colonel's face scrunched into a frown. "Dr. Jackson?"

"Long story," Daniel said, giving an involuntary flinch as a dart whined close overhead. "Can you run?"

"He can run." Teyla took a firm hold of Sheppard's arm. "Let's go."

As Teyla pulled Sheppard along, Daniel hung back, peering through the dark toward the repository as he caught his breath. Jack should have blown it by now. They should have heard the detonation.

"He's still got time," Beckett said, panting at Daniel's shoulder. "You need to trust him."

"I do. I trust him to blow it, but…" He shook his head. Too late now, the die was cast.

"Doctors?" Novak called from a couple steps ahead. "Move it along."

Daniel nodded and broke into a jog, Beckett huffing at his side.

"You think Jack's got nothing to live for?" Beckett said as he ran, each word rattling in his chest.

"He's said as much."

"Aye, well," Beckett huffed. "Things change."

Not that fast, Daniel thought. Beckett hadn't seen Jack before they came here, angry and bitter and ready to spill his blood on the streets of Raqqa if he thought it would make a difference. "I should have stayed with him," he said. "If the Wraith—"

"If the Wraith take the damn gate," Novak interrupted. "None of us are getting outa here. Now move it, Doctors."

Beckett grabbed Daniel's arm, getting his attention as they slalomed through the trees, mere shadows in the gloom. "Let Jack do his job, son. Trust him. He'll come through."

Daniel could only hope that he wanted to.

The trick would be to set the timer for long enough to get the Wraith into the room, but not long enough for them to be able to disable it. Which meant leaving it until the last moment, until he could practically see the whites—yellows?—of their eyes.

He could hear them in the complex, their heavy boots on the stone floor. No shouting, though, no barked commands like with the Goa'uld. Silent, alien. And yet they were oddly human, in some ways. More so than the snake-heads with their clownish posturing and over-the-top Bad Guy personas. The concern he'd seen for the Wraith kid was like nothing he'd ever seen the Goa'uld exhibit.

These Wraith were something else entirely.

Crouched next to the C4, he toggled the detonator to one minute and waited before setting it. It would be cutting it fine to get out and he'd have a long and lonely flight to the gate, but he could do it. In this young man's body, he could do it with no problem. His former self… He allowed a brief smile at the thought of General O'Neill high-tailing it back to the Stargate.

And then he stopped. Because although O'Neill might be slower, at least he'd be running toward home. But what waited for him on the other side of the Stargate? Atlantis and then…?

He knew enough about the NID, the military, and his place within it to understand that he wouldn't be walking free and he wouldn't be rejoining the SGC. He was too big of a liability and too big of an asset—and they owned his ass. He knew that too.

Wraith footsteps drew closer, a careful predatory tread. It was time to go, to make is break for…what? He couldn't call it freedom. But he'd told Daniel the truth: he wasn't planning to die here.

One minute. He set the timer.

Go.

On silent feet, he crept to the dark opening of the corridor leading to the back door. He was, perhaps, three seconds too slow.

The Wraith hissed from the doorway on the other side of the chamber and Jack dived back and to the side, the stunner blast missing him by inches. Crap.

He squeezed off two shots from his berretta, both hitting their mark. The Wraith lurched back, but didn't go down.

Jack ran.

He could hear the thing behind him, its pounding footsteps and savage snarl, and when it grabbed the back of his jacket Jack was ready. He flung himself back into the Wraith, knocking them both off balance and into the wall, then brought his elbow back hard into its gut and slammed its head into the wall.

But the bastard was strong, one hand wrapping around Jack's arm and slamming him face-first into the opposite wall, knocking his weapon out of his hand before it turned him around and pressed up him against the wall with one clawed hand around his throat. His feet barely touched the ground.

It snarled, baring its teeth, head cocked in an alien birdlike tilt. "Lantean," it hissed.

"Minnesotan, actually."

Another snarl as it lifted its right hand, baring a weird gaping maw in the palm of its hand. Jack had a nasty feeling he knew what that thing was for and tried to lurch away, but it had him fast. And in that moment, he knew it was true: he *didn't* want to die here. He wanted to take those second chances he'd ignored. He wanted every sunrise and every sunset. He wanted another chance at fatherhood, he wanted old age and bad knees. He wanted life.

"Sonofabitch," he growled and grabbed its hand with both of his own, holding it at bay.

*Five seconds*, he thought. He had to keep the thing off him for five more seconds…

"I will enjoy this, Lantean," the Wraith hissed close to his face, his arm descending towards Jack's chest despite his grip on it.

Jack bared his own teeth in a grimace. "Yes," he snarled, "you and me both, pal."

And then the C4 detonated, the blast hammering down the narrow corridor. Jack was ready for it, the Wraith wasn't. It stumbled, its grip loosened, and Jack grabbed its stunner, pressed it under the Wraith's chin and fire twice.

The thing jerked back, dead-eyed, and fell, leaving Jack gasping.

Stone-dust clogged the air, Jack coughed, spat and staggered into a run. Daniel would be holding the gate open, he knew he would, and all Jack had to do was reach it.

Piece of cake.

Colonel Sam Carter stood in the operations room in Atlantis, eyes fixed on the open gate as Colonel Novak's team piled through.

One man was down, carried limp between his team-mates. Dr. Beckett was already treating him as they pulled the man away from the gate, calling for a med team. Then came Teyla and Ronon at a dead run, helping Sheppard, followed a moment later by Novak. He was cursing a blue-streak, turning angrily back to the gate as they waited.

And waited.

Daniel was still out there and Sam felt the usual tightening in the pit of her stomach. It was such a familiar sensation after all these years that she barely paid it any attention, just kept her eyes fixed on the event horizon and waited. Daniel was out there and so was Jack.

That was more complex. So was her reason for being here. General O'Neill's not-quite-orders sat heavily on her shoulders. The truth was, she'd hoped to avoid this meeting. It would be difficult for both of them.

She took in another breath, shoulders braced. The wormhole rippled and Daniel all but fell through, followed a moment later by two Wraith and Jack O'Neill carrying a child—a Wraith child—in his arms.

Sam let herself smile, half in relief and half in nostalgia, because of course Jack O'Neill would step through the gate holding the enemy's child in his arms. Some things never changed.

Daniel's hands were up, warning off the SFs who'd reacted instantly to the sight of the Wraith. Novak was barking orders too as the wormhole collapsed, cutting off its blue light.

Sam turned, put a hand on the shoulder of the airman sitting at his post next to her. "Please ask O'Neill to report to the *Hammond* once he's been debriefed," she said and, with a final look down at the gate, walked away to prepare for this inevitable meeting.

They'd given him quarters in Atlantis—fancy quarters with a view to die for over an endless ocean. It certainly beat the VIP quarters at the SGC. Jack tried not to consider it a jail, even if there were SFs outside the door.

He'd had time to shower and change and got the distinct and itchy feeling that he was waiting for something. He just wasn't sure what. The other shoe to drop, perhaps?

So it didn't surprise him when Daniel showed up at the door, murmuring quietly to the SFs as he stepped inside. "Hey," he said, hands deep in his pockets and watching Jack from over the rims of his glasses. "So, here we are again."

"Again?"

Daniel waved a hand between them. "Figuring out what happens next."

"You say it like I have a choice in the matter."

Daniel glanced down, like he couldn't meet Jack's eyes. "I, uh, listen," he said. "Sam's here."

Jack felt a treacherous lurch in the pit of his stomach, but managed to keep it out of his voice. "Oh," he said.

"She just arrived on the *Hammond*."

"And you're telling me this because…?"

"Because she needs to talk to you." Daniel nodded up at the ceiling, past the ceiling. "On the *Hammond*."

Jack turned away to look out the window so that Daniel couldn't see his face. He didn't exactly trust himself on this subject. "About what?"

"I don't know," Daniel said. "I think— I understand it's on General O'Neill's orders."

He snorted a laugh. "Ironic."

Daniel's answering hum in the back of his throat was entirely noncommittal. "You want me to come with you?"

It might not be a bad idea, he thought, but perhaps that was the cowardly response. "I think I can handle Carter," he said, turning back around with a flat smile.

Daniel just nodded. "Yeah. Okay."

"Do you think I'll come back?" he said then.

"Back?"

"Do you think this is my one-way ticket to Earth? Go straight to jail, do not pass go?"

Daniel frowned, the expression creasing the space between his eyebrows. "No. I don't think— Jack, it's Sam. Whatever this is, you know she's got your back."

All Jack really trusted was that Daniel believed it, but Jack had made his choice when he'd walked back through the

Stargate to Atlantis, when he'd chosen to live, and there was no going back now. Spreading his arms— no time like the present—he said, "So. Beam me up, Scotty."

Daniel smiled, toggled his earpiece, and said, "He's ready."

Which, Jack thought as the world shimmered around him, was a gross overstatement. Ready was the very last thing he was.

A moment later he found himself on the bridge of a pretty spectacular ship, the wide view-screen filled with stars and the arc of the planet below. A woman he didn't recognize introduced herself as Lieutenant Ashok, and said, "Colonel Carter's waiting for you, sir."

Jack raised an eyebrow at the 'sir', but didn't comment. "Lead the way," he said, and tried to work some moisture into his mouth. He hadn't seen Carter for ten years. He had no idea what to expect.

He followed Ashok along a narrow corridor and allowed himself to be impressed. That this ship was theirs, Earth's, was incredibly cool. That Carter was in command was— Well, not exactly surprising but certainly impressive. But, of course, Carter had never done anything but impress him.

Ashok stopped outside a doorway, knocked and waited. Jack quashed a ridiculous instinct to come to attention.

A voice—Carter's voice—said, "Come in" and Ashok gave Jack a nod as she opened the door for him and stood back.

Taking a deep breath, Jack stepped inside. And there she was, getting up from behind her desk with a nervous smile. "Jack," she said as the door closed behind him. "It's good to see you."

"Carter." He didn't approach, felt the need to keep his distance. "Long time no see."

She nodded and came around to the front of her desk, perching on the edge. She was older, of course. He could see it around her eyes, but she wore it well, wore her new authority well. "This— This is very strange. It must be for you too."

"Strange is kinda normal these days," he said, taking a glance around the room. It was obviously an office with a few personal possessions dotted here and there. He could make out an old photo of SG1 on a shelf behind her desk—him, or the other version of him—included. Next to it was another frame, set face down on the shelf. He wondered what it was, why she didn't want him to see it. He could guess, of course, but steered his mind away from that channel.

"I hear you brought some new friends back from M67-2Y5."

"Well," he said, meeting and holding her gaze, "you know me and leaving people behind."

She flinched at that, but didn't look away. "We all did what we thought was best," she said and he could hear ten years of command in the authority in her voice. "I think you know that, Jack."

Instead of answering, because he knew she was right, he said, "So, nice as this is, Carter, you want to tell me why I'm here?"

"Okay. Down to business, then."

Jack lifted an eyebrow. "What else is there?"

She gave a tight smile, a little irritated, very Carter. "I have an offer from General O'Neill. He's—" She broke off to consider her words. "He's been made aware, off the record, that the IOA has plans for you."

"If it includes any kind of probe…"

Another flash of a smile. "They think you're dangerous, Jack, a loose cannon that needs to be brought back under control." Her smile vanished, pressed into a thin-lipped expression. "They want you on a very short leash—possibly at Groom Lake, maybe military intelligence."

"And if that's not an oxymoron…" He held up a hand when Carter made to speak again. "Look, I get it, Carter. So cut to the chase. Why are you here? To take me back?"

"Yes. If you want."

"If I *want* to?" He narrowed his eyes. "Are you saying I have a choice?"

She paused for a beat, glanced away from him and to somewhere in the middle distance. "The general… He's suggested we, to quote, 'Leave it like Abydos.'" Her gaze met his. "You understand?"

"Bury the gate? Euphemistically speaking?"

"If that's what you want."

"And I'd stay here on Atlantis?"

Carter shook her head. "We can't involve the Atlantis expedition in this--well, not officially. But there are places here where you'd find a welcome. Ronon's world, Sateda, is rebuilding. They're good people, they need all the help they can get. Or Teyla's people, the Athosians…" She gave a slight smile. "They're traders. Plenty of time for fishing on New Athos, I understand."

He caught the allusion, let it curl painful around his chest. "You, ah, you ever make it up to the cabin?"

After a pause she nodded. "Yeah," she said, holding his gaze with a complex expression. "Yeah, we did. It's beautiful."

Jack swallowed and looked away. "I miss it. All of it."

Carter let out a slow breath. "I'd understand if you want to take your chances with the NID. After time, they might let you—"

"You know Beckett?" Jack said. "The doc?"

"Of course."

"You know he's, uh…"

"A clone? Yes."

"He's made a life here," Jack said. "A different life from what he had—from what he was. It got me thinking."

"That you could have a new life here too?"

"No, that— That I already have a new life, that I'm not *him* anymore. I'm not the Jack O'Neill you knew ten years ago."

After a pause, Carter nodded. "You're right. You're— You seem different. You talk different, you look—"

"Better, right? It's the hair."

Carter smiled. "Just different."

He let the silence settle between them for a moment, then

said, "So I guess the question is what I do with this new life. I'm not spending it as the NID's pet rat."

"So we bury the gate."

"Which means?"

She gave him a flat smile. "You're a very ingenious person, Jack. Given the right circumstances, I'm sure you could find your way to one of the *Hammond's* 302s. We'd probably have a hard time tracking your flight path, especially if our scanners were off-line for routine maintenance."

Jack felt his eyebrows rise. "And exactly how big of a heap of steaming crap would you get into for letting *that* happen under your command?"

"That's not your concern."

"Carter—"

"We're family, Jack: you, me, Daniel and Teal'c. Do you think there's anything we wouldn't do for you?"

He looked at her for a moment, too much welling up to contain. "Just—" He took a breath and held out his arms. "C'mere, Sam."

After a beat she stepped into his embrace, wrapped her arms around him. He knew they were saying goodbye, that this was both goodbye and forgiveness. "I'm sorry," she said, breathing the words into his shoulder. "I wish things had turned out better for you."

Jack took a breath, steadied himself, and said, "Who says they won't?" He pulled away to look at her. "Also, I have a better plan."

"A better plan?"

He smiled. "I just need a little time with our space-vampire friends."

General Jack O'Neill rose as the door to his office opened. "Colonel," he said, schooling his face not to smile. "It's good to have you home."

"Thank you, sir."

He nodded to the man sitting across the desk from him. "Mr. Coolidge, this is Colonel Carter."

They exchanged formalities and Jack sat down, Carter following. "The *Hammond* just got back a couple hours ago," he told Coolidge, "but I wanted Carter to brief you on this before I take it to the IOA."

Coolidge folded his hands on his lap. "Very well."

Clearing her throat, Carter passed Jack a slim manila folder. "There was an incident on Atlantis," she said. "During the mission to retrieve Colonel Sheppard, the team brought two Wraith and their sick child to Atlantis. Dr. Beckett was able to help the child but, unfortunately, once the child was well the Wraith attempted to kidnap Dr. Beckett so that he could continue his treatment of the girl. There was a firefight and Jack O'Neill—the clone—was killed rescuing Dr. Beckett." She sat up straighter, shoulders braced. "I'm sorry to report that he was fed on by the Wraith."

"That is very concerning," Coolidge said. "His body has been returned to Earth, I assume?"

"Unfortunately," Carter said, with a perfect poker face, "the Wraith discarded his body over the side of the city after it had fed. We were unable to retrieve it. The ocean is very deep."

Coolidge was silent, nodding in thought. "That is a tragic end for a man with— With such a troubled past. I hope he finds peace. In the next world, of course."

"Yes," Carter said. "I hope so too."

Pushing himself to his feet, Coolidge turned to O'Neill. "Thank you, General. Obviously the IOA will be displeased, but…" A trace of a smile touched his mouth. "What's done is done. They will, no doubt, review your decision to send the clone to Atlantis in the first place."

Jack spread his hands on the desk, then stood up too. "I'll look forward to it," he said with a smile.

With a nod, Coolidge left. Carter started to follow, but Jack held her back with a touch to her wrist. "Everything okay?" he said quietly, reaching past her to close the door.

"Yes, sir. Daniel can fill us in when he gets back. He, um, stayed to do a little additional research."

"Ah," Jack smiled. "Research."

"On Sateda. Interestingly, they're looking for pilots there—to help locate any outlying communities that survived the culling."

"That *is* interesting."

She smiled. "Yes, sir."

Looking past her, through the glass walls of his office, he saw his assistant talking to Colonel Turner, his next meeting. With a sigh, Jack glanced at Carter. "We'll catch up later?"

"Looking forward to it," she said, dropping the sir with a smile.

He let out a breath. "It's good to have you home, Sam."

# EPILOGUE

IN THE BRIGHT morning light, Daniel squinted across the plaza that housed the Satedan Stargate. The buildings on all sides of the square bore the signs of war and dereliction, but they were all under construction now and bustling with people.

This was a world in the process of being reborn, of returning to life. A place of hope. It was profoundly inspiring. And it felt like the right place for Jack—this young, not-quite-hopeful Jack. He watched as the man in question walked toward him, dressed in a mish-mash of his SGC uniform and the native clothes of the planet. Somehow he'd finagled a pair of sunglasses and he looked a lot like the man Daniel had once known, all bluster and swagger as he strode across the square. It made Daniel smile.

"Hey," Jack said as he approached. "You heading out, then?"

"Papers to write, meetings to sleep through," Daniel said. "How about you? Are you flying today?"

"Every day I can," Jack grinned. Properly grinned. It was disconcerting seeing that smile on his face, so different from his own Jack O'Neill. If he didn't already know it, it would be proof that these were two different men growing increasingly distinct as time passed. Which was a good thing, he reminded himself. A healthy thing.

As if he was reading his thoughts, Jack said, "I like this place. It's— I've spent a lot of time in war zones, Daniel. It feels good to be somewhere on the other side of it, somewhere getting better instead of worse."

"You can do good here," Daniel agreed. "And I think it'll do you good too."

"Yeah, maybe." Then he frowned. "Hey, did you hear back from Fangs?"

Daniel quirked a smile. "Um, if you mean the Wraith, then

no. But the Wraith aren't exactly ones for keeping in touch."

Jack shrugged. "I hope the kid's okay."

"Carson thinks she should be," Daniel said. "But it's interesting, the idea of cloning a Queen. It could— Well, she's young. I guess we'll see."

Pulling off his sunglasses, Jack squinted at him. "But it could have consequences?"

Daniel shrugged. "Every choice has consequences, right? And who knows whether they'll be good or bad?"

Jack's attention darted past Daniel as, behind him, someone shouted and the gate started grinding into life. "So… Your cue," Jack said.

"Yeah. Guess this is it, then."

"It's not 'it'," Jack said. "It's just 'see you later'."

"I don't exactly get to Sateda very often."

"But you will," Jack said, and there was enough earnest hope in his voice to tell Daniel he needed a promise.

"I will. And, listen, if you ever need anything, get in touch. We have friends on Atlantis. They'll get a message to us. Beckett, Ronon, Teyla… Even McKay, probably."

"Last resort," Jack said with a smile, "but okay."

With a whoosh the gate opened, its light dazzled by the morning sun. Reaching out, Daniel pulled Jack into a hug. "Take care of yourself, Jack."

"Nah," Jack said, hugging him back. "I plan to be young and reckless. For a while, at least."

Daniel laughed, knocked his fist against Jack's back a couple times, and then stood back. "In that case, have fun," he said. "You've earned it."

Jack's answering smile faded, turning serious. "Thanks Daniel," he said. "I mean — You know, for this. For everything."

"Yeah. I know."

He turned on the steps to the gate, took one last look at Jack O'Neill—young and vital in the morning sunlight—and felt his heart soar. This felt like a new beginning, like cosmic payback for all that Jack O'Neill had done for the galaxy.

And for once he thought Jack might let himself look for the happiness he deserved.

# STARGÅTE SG·1

# STARGATE ATLANTIS

## Original novels based on the hit TV shows STARGATE SG-1 and STARGATE ATLANTIS

Available as e-books from leading online retailers

Paperback editions available from Amazon and IngramSpark

If you liked this book, please tell your friends and leave a review on a bookstore website. Thanks!